A Small Person Far Away

For a moment she remembered exactly what it had felt like. It was as though, for a fraction of a second, she had half-seen, half-become the small, fierce, vulnerable person she had once been, with her lace-up boots and socks held up by elastic bands, her fear of volcanoes and of dying in the night, her belief that rust caused blood poisoning, liquorice was made of horses' blood, and there would never be another war, and her unshakeable conviction that there was no problem in the world that Mama could not easily solve.

The small person did not say, "Is Mama home?" She said, "Ist Mami da?" and did not speak a word of English, and for a moment Anna felt shaken by her sudden emergence.

Also by Judith Kerr

When Hitler Stole Pink Rabbit
The Other Way Round

*All three titles are also available
in a single volume:*

Out of the Hitler Time

Judith Kerr

A Small Person Far Away

Collins
An *Imprint of* HarperCollins*Publishers*

First published in Great Britain by
William Collins Sons & Company Ltd. in 1978.
First published in Lions in 1993 and
reprinted by Collins in 1995.
7 9 8

Collins is an imprint of HarperCollins*Publishers* Ltd,
77-85 Fulham Palace Road,
Hammersmith, London W6 8JB.

ISBN 0 00 671704-7

Printed and bound in Great Britain by
Caledonian International Book Manufacturing Ltd, Glasgow G64

For my husband

Saturday

The rug was exactly the right red – not too orange and not too purple, but that lovely glowing shade between the two which was so difficult to find. It would look marvellous in the dining-room.

"I'd like it, please," said Anna. Clearly it was her lucky day.

She glanced at her reflection in a glass-fronted show-case full of table linen as the assistant led her to his desk. Her green coat – not passed on to her by friends but bought by herself – hung easily from her shoulders. The printed silk scarf, the well-cut dark hair and the reasonably confident expression were all in keeping with the status of the store around her. A well-heeled young Englishwoman out shopping. Well, she thought, nowadays I suppose that's what I am.

While she wrote out a cheque and the assistant copied her name and address for the rug's delivery, she imagined telling Richard about it. It would make their flat almost complete. All that was needed now were little things like cushions and lampshades, and perhaps, if Richard finished his script soon, they would be able to choose those together.

She became aware of the assistant hesitating over her name on the cheque.

"Excuse me asking, madam," he said, "but is that any relation to the gentleman who writes for television?"

"My husband," she said and felt the usual fatuous, self-congratulatory grin spread over her face as she said it. Ridiculous, she thought. I should be used to it by now.

"Really?" The assistant's face was pink with pleasure. "I must tell the wife. We watch all his plays, you know. Wherever does he get his ideas from, madam? Do you help him at all with his writing?"

Anna laughed. "No," she said. "He helps me."

"Really? Do you write as well then?"

Why did I ever start on this? she thought. "I work in television," she said. "But mostly I just rewrite little bits of other people's plays. And if I get stuck, I ask my husband when I get home."

The assistant, after considering this, rightly dismissed it. "When that big serial of his was on last year," he said, "the wife and I stayed home for it every Saturday night. So did just about everyone else our way. It was so exciting – not like anything we'd ever seen."

Anna nodded and smiled. It had been Richard's first great success.

"We got married on the strength of that," she said.

She remembered the register office in Chelsea, next to the foot clinic. Richard's parents down from the north of England, Mama over from Berlin, their own friends from the BBC, cousin Otto passing out at the reception and saying it was the heat, but it had really been the champagne. And then the taxi coming and Richard and herself driving off and leaving them all behind.

"It was quite exciting for us too," she said.

When she walked out of the store into Tottenham Court Road, the world exploded into noise and light. A new building was going up next door and the sunshine trembled with the din of pneumatic drills. One of the workmen had taken off his shirt in spite of the October chill and winked at her as she passed. Behind him the last remains of a bombed building, scraps of wallpaper still adhering to the bricks and plaster, crumbled to a bulldozer. Soon there would be no bomb damage at all left visible in London. And about time too, she thought, eleven years after the war.

She crossed the road to get away from the noise. Here the shops were more or less unchanged – shabby and haphazard, selling things you could not imagine anyone wanting to buy. The Woolworth's, too, was much as she remembered it. She had come here with Mama when they had first arrived in England as refugees from Hitler, and Mama had bought herself a pair of silk stockings for a shilling. Later when Papa could no longer earn any money, Mama had been reduced to buying the stockings one at a time for sixpence, and even though they were supposed to be all the same colour, they had never quite matched.

"If only, just once, I could buy myself two stockings together," she had cried.

And now here was Anna buying expensive rugs, and Mama earning dollars back in Germany, as though none of the hardships had ever happened. Only Papa had not lived to see everything change.

For a moment she considered trying to find the boarding house somewhere nearby which had been her first English home, but decided against it. It had been bombed during the Blitz and would probably be unrecognizable anyway. Once she had tried to show Richard the other boarding house in Putney where they had moved after the bomb, but had found it replaced by three skimpy family dwellings with identical tree-less lawns and crazy-paving. The only thing that had been the same was the bench at the end of the street where Papa had sometimes sat in the sun with his pipe. He had eked out the tobacco with dried leaves and rose petals, and for lunch he had eaten bread toasted over the gas ring and spread with exactly one seventh of a jar of fish paste. If only he could have lived to see all this, thought Anna, as she passed a wine shop crammed with bottles – how he would have enjoyed it.

Oxford Street was bustling with Saturday shoppers. Should she walk through to Liberty's for a look at their lamps? But a number 73 bus stopped just as she was passing and she jumped on, climbed to the top deck and sat with the sun warming her face, visualizing the new rug in their tiny dining-room and planning what to wear to go out that evening, while the bus made its slow way through the traffic.

Outside Selfridges people were staring up at a brightly coloured plaster figure which was being hoisted into place above the main entrance. "Come and see Uncle Holly and his grotto of dwarfs," read posters in every window. Heavens, she thought, they're getting ready for Christmas already.

In Hyde Park, clearly making for Speakers' Corner, a small procession moved briskly under the thinning plane trees. Its members carried handmade placards with "Russians out of Hungary" on them, and one had mounted that morning's newspaper on a piece of cardboard. It showed a photograph of Russian tanks under the headline "Ring of Steel round Budapest". Most of them looked like students, but a few elderly people in dark old-fashioned clothes were probably Hungarian refugees. One of them, a man in a shabby coat with a pale, clever face reminded Anna of Papa.

At Knightsbridge the traffic thinned a little, and as the bus rolled past Kensington Gardens, she could see the leaves floating down from the trees on to the grass below, where groups of school children, urged on by their teachers, were playing football and rounders.

She got off at the bottom of Kensington Church Street and set off on her way home through the tree-lined residential streets at the foot of Camden Hill. Here there were almost no cars and few people. Cooking smells wafted across shrubby front gardens. A baby slept in its pram. Cats dozed on walls and pavements, and the falling leaves were everywhere. One drifted down quite close to her. She stretched up and caught it in mid-air. That means more luck, she thought, remembering a childhood superstition. For a moment she held it in her hand. Then she loosened her fingers and watched it spiral down to mingle with the others on the ground.

The block of flats where she and Richard lived was brand-new, and as soon as she could see it from the corner of the street, she automatically started to hurry. This always happened: she knew it was silly after being married for more than a year, but she still did it. She ran across the road, up the stone steps and along the red brick terrace so thick with leaves that she almost slipped. Outside the porter's flat below, the porter was talking to a boy on a bicycle. He waved when he saw her and called something that she did not catch, but she was in too much of a rush to stop. The lift was not there and, rather than wait for it, she ran up the two flights of stairs, opened the door with her key, and there was Richard.

He was sitting at his typewriter, much, as she had left him hours earlier. There a neat stack of paper on the table before him and a collection of crumpled pages overflowing from the wastepaper basket on to the floor. Behind him in the tiny living-room she could see their new striped sofa, the little red chair she had bought the previous week, and the curtains made from material designed by herself in her art school days. The vivid colours set off his dark hair and pale, restless face as he frowned at the paper, typing furiously with two fingers.

Normally she would not have interrupted him, but she felt too happy to wait. She let him get to the end of a line. Then she said, "It's lovely out. I've been all over town. And I've found a rug for the dining-room."

"Really?" He came back slowly from whatever world he had been writing about.

"And the man in the shop had seen all your plays on the telly and practically asked me for my autograph when he found out I was married to you."

He smiled. "There's fame!"

"Are you right in the middle of something?"

She saw him glance at the page in his typewriter and resign himself to abandoning it for the present. "I suppose it's lunch time. Anyway, I've got quite a bit done." He stood up and stretched. "What's the rug like? Is it the right red?"

She was beginning to describe it to him when the door bell rang. ". . . exactly what we were looking for," she said, and opened the door to find the porter outside.

"Telegram," he said and handed it over. It was for her. She knew it must be good news, for it was that sort of a day, and opened it quickly. And then, for a moment, everything seemed to stop.

For some strange reason she could see Richard quite clearly with part of her mind, even though her eyes were on the print. She heard him say, "What is it?" and after what seemed like an enormous gap of time of which she could later remember nothing but which could not really have lasted more than a few seconds, she pushed it into his hand.

"I don't understand it," she said. "Mama is never ill."

He spread it on the table and she read it again, hoping that she had got it wrong the first time.

"YOUR MOTHER SERIOUSLY ILL WITH PNEUMONIA STOP YOUR PRESENCE MAY BE NEEDED STOP PLEASE BOOK PROVISIONAL FLIGHT TOMORROW STOP WILL TELEPHONE NINE O'CLOCK TONIGHT." It was signed Konrad.

"All she's ever had is 'flu," said Anna. She felt that if she tried hard enough, she would be able to disprove the whole thing. She said, "I don't want to go to Berlin."

Then she found she was sitting down with Richard beside her. His face was troubled and she thought illogically that she shouldn't be distracting him in this way from his work. He tightened his arm round her shoulders.

"It's only a provisional booking," he said. "You may not need to go. By the time Konrad rings up, she may be better."

Of course, she thought, of course. She tried to remember what Konrad was like. During the years Mama had known him he had always seemed ultra-responsible. Probably he would act even on the off-chance of trouble. By tonight Mama might be sitting up in bed, her blue eyes outraged. For heaven's sake, Konrad, she would cry, why on earth did you cable the children?

"D'you suppose he's cabled Max as well?" she asked. Max was her brother, at present in Greece.

Richard shook his head. "Goodness knows." Then he said suddenly, "Would you like me to come with you?"

She was both touched and horrified. "Of course not. Not in the middle of your serial. Anyway, what could you do in Berlin?"

He made a face. "I wish I could speak German."

"It isn't that. But you know it would throw you completely to stop writing now. And Mama is my responsibility."

"I suppose so."

Eventually she rang Pan Am who were sympathetic when she explained the situation and said they would book her a seat. This seemed to make the whole thing more definite and she found herself suddenly close to tears.

"Come on," said Richard, "You need a drink." He poured her some of the whisky they normally kept for visitors and she gulped it down. "And food," he said. By the time they had made sandwiches and coffee and were sitting down to eat them in the little living-room, she felt better.

"But I still don't understand it," she said, clasping the hot mug for comfort. "Surely nowadays when people get pneumonia the doctors just fill them with penicillin? Unless the Germans haven't got it yet."

"They must have."

"Anyway, the Americans would have it, and they're the ones she works for. And how did she ever get pneumonia in the first place?"

Richard considered it. "Didn't she say something about sailing in her last letter? Perhaps if they'd had an accident – if she'd got very wet and cold and hadn't changed her clothes –"

"Konrad would make her."

For a moment they shared a vision of Konrad, solid and dependable, and Mama laughing and shouting, "It's only a bit of water." She always said a bit of water – it was one of the few mistakes she made in English. But perhaps she and Konrad spoke German together when they were alone. It astonished Anna that she had no idea whether they did or not.

"I'll see if I can find the letter," she said and

suddenly remembered something. "I don't believe I ever answered it."

"We haven't had it that long, have we?"

"I don't know."

The letter, when she uncovered it, turned out to be like most of Mama's – a fairly emphatic account of small successes in her work and social life. She had been chosen to go to Hanover for a few days in connection with her work, and she and Konrad had been invited to a Thanksgiving party by an American general. The only reference to sailing was that the weather was now too cold to do so, and that she and Konrad were playing a lot of bridge instead. It was exactly one month old.

"It doesn't matter, love," said Richard. "You'll be talking to Konrad tonight and if it's really serious you'll see your mother tomorrow."

"I know." But it still worried her. "I kept meaning to write," she said. "But with the flat and the new job –" Somehow she felt that a letter would have protected Mama from catching pneumonia.

"Well, no one can catch pneumonia from playing bridge," said Richard. "Not even your mother," and she laughed because it was true. Mama did everything to excess.

Suddenly, for no particular reason, she remembered Mama trying to buy her some boots when they had first come to England. Mama had walked her the whole length of Oxford Street from Tottenham Court Road to Marble Arch and they had gone into every shoe shop on the way. Anna had soon noticed that the various branches of Dolcis, Lilley and Skinner and Mansfield all had the same stock, but Mama had remained convinced that somehow, somewhere, there might be lurking a pair of boots just fractionally better or cheaper than any of the rest. When at last they bought some similar to the very first pair they had seen, Mama had said, "Well, at least we know that we haven't missed anything."

Mama could never bear to miss anything, real or imaginary, from a cheaper pair of boots to a day in the sun.

"She's a romantic," said Anna. "She always has been. I suppose Papa was too, but in a different way."

"What I've always found surprising is that she resented being a refugee so much more than he did," said Richard. "At least from what you've told me. After all, as a writer he really lost everything. Money, a great reputation and the language he wrote in." He looked troubled, as always when he talked about Papa. "I don't know how one could go on after that."

For a moment Anna saw Papa quite clearly in his shabby room, sitting at his rickety typewriter and smiling fondly, ironically, without a trace of self-pity. Reluctantly, she let the picture fade.

"It sounds odd," she said, "but in a way I think he found it interesting. And of course it was hard for Mama because she had to cope with the practical things."

When Papa could no longer earn any money, Mama had supported the family with a series of secretarial jobs. Though she had learned neither shorthand nor typing, she had still managed, somehow, to reproduce approximately what had been dictated to her. She had survived, but she had hated it. At night, in the bedroom which she and Anna shared in the Putney boarding house, she had talked of all the things she had hoped to do in her life and now might never do. Sometimes when she set out for her boring work in the mornings, she was filled with such rage and despair that they made a kind of aura round her. Anna remembered that one of her employers, a man with slicked-down hair who dealt in third-rate clothing, had sacked her because, he said, just being in the same room with her made him feel exhausted. Mama had come home and cried and Anna had felt helpless and guilty, as though she ought to have been able to do something about it.

"It's such bad luck that this illness should have happened now," she said to Richard. "Just when everything is so much better for her at last."

She cleared away the lunch things while Richard picked at his script and then she looked out some clothes to pack, in case it should really be necessary for her to go to Berlin. For some reason the thought filled her with horror. Why? she thought. Why should I mind so much? She could not convince herself that Mama's illness was really dangerous, so it wasn't that. Rather it was a fear of going back. Back to Berlin? Back to Mama? Silly, she thought. It's not as though they could keep me there.

When she returned to the living-room, Richard was crumpling yet another page into the wastepaper basket.

"No good," he said. "Real life is too distracting." He looked at his watch. "What do you want to do till Konrad rings up?"

Something clicked in her memory. "Good heavens!" she cried. "We're supposed to go to the Dillons. I'd totally forgotten. I'd better ring him quickly."

"The Dillons? Oh," he said. "Drinks with the boss." He put out his hand as she reached for the telephone. "Don't cancel it. You'll have to tell him anyway if you go to Berlin."

James Dillon was head of the BBC Drama department and the invitation was to mark her promotion from editor to script writer.

"But we have to be here when Konrad rings."

"It's only a brisk walk. There's plenty of time. Come on," he said. "It'll be better than sitting here and brooding."

It was dark when they set out, and suddenly cold with a thin drizzle of rain. She pulled her coat tight about her and let Richard lead her through the network of quiet streets. Though Richard had met James Dillon's family before, she had never been to their house. Her promotion had been James Dillon's idea, but it was Richard who had originally encouraged her to write. When they had first met, he had read a short story she had written in between the paintings which she considered her real work. "This is good," he had said. "You must do more."

At first it had seemed like cheating, for though words came to her fairly easily ("Runs in the family," Richard had said), she had set her heart on being a painter. But no one seemed eager to buy her pictures, whereas she had no trouble at all in landing a minor job in television. By the time she and Richard were married, she was editing plays, and now here she was, officially a script writer. It had all happened so quickly that she still thought of it as his world rather than hers. "I hope I can really do this job," she said, and then, "What's James Dillon's wife like?"

"Nice," he said. "Don't worry."

They were reaching the end of a narrow side street and became aware of many voices and footsteps ahead of them. As they turned into the brightness of Notting Hill Gate, they found themselves suddenly surrounded by a great crowd. In spite of the rain which had begun to fall in earnest, a mass of people blocked the pavement, overflowing into the gutter, and were moving slowly but determinedly all in the same direction. In the road beyond, two policemen were trying to keep a space between the crowd and the passing cars. For a moment Anna and Richard were swept along with the rest.

"Who are they?" said Richard, and then they saw, swaying in the darkness above them, the pale handwritten placards.

"It must be Hungary again," said Anna. "I saw a procession in Hyde Park this morning."

At that moment the crowd slowed to a stop, and simultaneously a noisy party emerged from a pub nearby, causing a congestion. One of them, a large drunken looking woman, almost tripped and swore loudly.

"What the hell's this then?" she said, and another member of the group answered, "Bloody Hungary."

A placard bearer near Anna, an elderly man in dark clothes, mistook this exchange for interest in his cause and turned towards them. "The Russians kill our people," he explained with difficulty in a thick accent. "Many hundreds die each day. Please the English to help us . . ."

The woman stared incredulously. "Think we want another war?" she shouted. "I'm not having anyone drop bombs on my kids just for a lot of bloody foreigners!"

Just then the crowd began to move again and a gap opened between Anna and the kerb. "Come on," said Richard and pushed her through. They ran across Notting Hill Gate in the increasingly heavy rain, then zig-zagged through dark side streets on the other side until they were standing outside a tall terrace house and Richard was ringing the bell. She only had time to take in an overgrown front garden with what looked like a pram under a tarpaulin, when the door was opened by a slight, pretty woman with untidy fair hair.

"Richard!" she cried. "And you must be Anna.

I'm Elizabeth. How lovely – we've been longing to see you."

She led the way through the narrow hall, edging with practised ease round a large balding teddy and a scooter leaning against the wall.

"Did you get caught up in the procession?" she called back as they followed her up the narrow stairs. "They've been demonstrating outside the Russian embassy all day. Poor souls, much good may it do them."

She suddenly darted sideways into a kitchen festooned with washing, where a small boy was eating cornflakes with a guinea pig squatting next to his dish.

"James thinks no one is going to lift a finger to help them. He thinks it's Munich all over again," she said as Anna and Richard caught up with her and, almost in the same breath to the little boy, "Darling, you won't forget to put Patricia back in her cage, will you. Remember how upset you were when Daddy nearly trod on her."

In the momentary silence while she snatched some ice cubes from the refrigerator into a glass bowl, the sound of two recorders, each playing a different tune and interspersed with wild childish giggles, drifted down from somewhere above.

"I'm afraid the girls are not really musical," she said and added, "Of course no one wants a third world war."

As they followed her out of the kitchen, Anna saw that the guinea pig was now slurping up cornflakes, its front paws in the dish, and the small boy called after them, "It wasn't Patricia's fault. Daddy should have looked!"

In the L shaped drawing-room next door James Dillon was waiting for them, his Roman emperor's face incongruous above the old sweater he was wearing instead of his usual BBC pinstripes. He kissed Anna and put an arm round Richard's shoulders, and when they were all settled with drinks, raised his glass.

"To you," he said. "To Richard's new serial which I'm sure will be as good as his first and to Anna's new job."

This was the cue she had nervously been waiting for. She said quickly, "I'm afraid I may not be able to start straight away," and explained about Mama's illness. The Dillons were immediately full of sympathy. James told her not to worry and to take as much time off as she liked and Elizabeth said, how awful for her but nowadays with penicillin pneumonia wasn't nearly as serious as it used to be. Then she said, "But whatever is your mother doing in Berlin?"

James said, "It's where you came from, isn't it?" and Anna explained that Mama was translating documents for the American Occupation Force and that, yes, she and her family had lived in Berlin until they had had to flee from the Nazis when she was nine.

"I didn't see any horrors," she said quickly, alarmed by more sympathy in Elizabeth's eyes. "My parents got us out before any of it happened. In fact, my brother and I rather enjoyed it. We lived in Switzerland and in France before we came here and we really liked all the different schools and different languages. But of course it was very hard for my parents, especially my father being a writer."

"Terrible." James shook his head, and Elizabeth asked, "And where is your father now?"

"Oh," said Anna, "he died soon after the war." She felt suddenly dangerously exposed. Something was rising up inside her and she began to talk very fast so as to keep it under. "He died in Hamburg," she almost gabbled. "Actually it was very strange because he'd never been back to Germany since we left. But the British Control Commission asked him to write about the German theatre which was just starting up again. He'd been famous as a drama critic before Hitler, you see, and I think it was supposed to be good for German morale."

She paused, but the Dillons were both looking at her, absorbed in the story, and she had to continue.

"They flew him over – he'd never flown but he loved it. I don't think he knew quite what to expect when he got there, but when he stepped off the plane, there were reporters and photographers waiting for him. And then a great lunch with speeches, and a tour of the city. And when he walked into the theatre that evening the audience stood up and applauded. I suppose it was all too much for him. Anyway –" She glanced at Richard, suddenly horribly unsure if she could go on. "He had a stroke and died a few weeks later. My mother was with him, but we . . . my brother and I . . ."

Richard put his hand over hers and said, "I've always been so sorry that I never knew him. Or read him. It seems he's untranslatable," and the Dillons, after James had refilled her glass, tactfully embarked on a discussion of translations in general and that of a recent French play in particular.

She was grateful for Richard's hand and for not having to talk. She had not expected to be so upset. After all it had happened years ago. It was the thought of how it had happened, of course. She remembered Papa's coffin draped with the Union Jack. Common practice, they had said for a British subject dying abroad. It had seemed strange, for Papa had never managed to speak English properly and had been a British subject only for the last year of his life. Then the icy hall where the German musicians had played Beethoven's Seventh which Papa had loved so much, and the British soldiers who, together with Max and a local newspaperman, had helped to carry his coffin.

As Papa had planned.

If Mama died, it wouldn't be like that. Anyway, Mama couldn't die. She was too strong. Anna suddenly remembered with total clarity how Mama had looked when she and Max had arrived, stunned, in Hamburg.

"*Bitte etwas Tee.*" Tea in the hotel bedroom,

the only warm place in the devastated city. Mama saying, "There is something I must tell you about Papa."

As though anything else could possibly matter, Anna had thought, apart from the fact that Papa was dead. Then Mama talking about how Papa had failed to recover from the effects of the stroke. But they knew that already. Something about German doctors. How you could get anything for a packet of cigarettes. What?? Anna had thought. What??

"He was paralysed and in pain. He felt he could no longer think as clearly as he wished. I'd always promised to help him if that happened."

The sharp intake of breath from Max beside her. Mama's eyes shifting minutely towards him.

"So I did what he asked. I helped him."

She had said it in such matter of fact tones that even then Anna had not immediately understood.

"It was what he wanted." Mama had stared at them both, white faced and steely.

Max had said in a forlorn voice, "But we never said goodbye to him."

She could not remember what she herself had said. But she had known with complete certainty that what Mama had done was right.

She became aware of Richard looking at her. As usual, he knew what she was thinking. She sent him a reassuring look back and tried to listen to the conversation which seemed to have moved on from the French play to a discussion of its author.

James Dillon said something witty and everyone laughed. Elizabeth, relaxed in her chair, brushed a strand of hair out of her face. She thought, I am the only person in this room to whom such things have happened. I don't want to be. I want to belong here.

"Of course the French system of education . . ."

"What was it like being a child in Paris?"

She realized that Elizabeth was addressing her.

"In Paris? Oh –" She made an effort and began to talk about her school, the teacher called Madame Socrate who had helped her learn French, the friends she had made, outings to the country and to celebrate the 14th July. "I loved it," she said and found herself smiling.

"Of course you did." James Dillon had risen and she saw that he was wearing his Head of Drama expression which she knew from the BBC. "Now here's what we're going to do. If your mother needs you, you'll go and cope with whatever has to be done. And when you come back you'll do that adaptation we talked about. But I'd like you also to think about writing something of your own."

For the first time she was startled into total attention. "Of my own?"

"Why not? Needn't be very long, but all your own work." He raised his extravagant eyebrows. "Might be interesting."

It was so good to think about coming back from Berlin rather than going away that she tried to stifle her doubts about writing something original.

"All right," she said. "Though I'm not absolutely sure . . ."

"Think about it," said James.

She was saved from having to say anything more by the arrival of the small boy with the guinea pig clutched to his chest. After being introduced, he wandered over to his mother and allowed himself to be hugged. Then he whispered in her ear, was told not to whisper and said loudly, "Can Patricia have a crisp?"

"I didn't know she liked crisps," said Elizabeth.

"I don't know either." His small face furrowed as he searched for the right word. "It's an experiment," he said precisely.

He was given a potato crisp from a dish and they all watched while the guinea pig sniffed it in a corner of the floor and finally decided to crunch it up.

"She likes it," said the child, pleased.

"Go and get a saucer," said Elizabeth. "Then you and Patricia can have some crisps all to yourselves."

"All right." He scooped up the guinea pig. "Come on, Patricia," he said. "You're going to have . . ." He hesitated, but as he got to the door they heard him say happily, "A banquet."

In the quiet after he'd gone, Anna could hear the recorders, now both on the same tune, from the floor above.

"He's got quite a vocabulary," said Richard. "How old is he?"

"Six," said Elizabeth. Clearly he was the apple of their eye.

"Loves words," said James. "Been reading since he was four. Taken to writing stories now."

"Most of them about Patricia," giggled Elizabeth. "I bet you didn't know guinea pigs can pilot aeroplanes." She stopped as the child reappeared and helped him fill a saucer with crisps. Then she was struck by a thought. "I do find it absolutely extraordinary," she said to Anna, "that when you were his age you were speaking nothing but German. Can you still speak it?"

"A bit," said Anna. "I've forgotten a lot of it."

Elizabeth handed the child the saucer. "This lady has forgotten nearly all the words she knew when she was your age, can you imagine?" she said. "And she's learned a whole lot of new ones instead."

He stared at Anna in disbelief. Then he said, "I wouldn't."

"Wouldn't what?" asked his father.

"Forget." He saw everyone looking at him and took a deep breath. "I wouldn't forget the words I know. Even if – even if I learned a million trillion new words. I'd always remember."

"Well, it would only be if you went to a place where no one spoke English," said James. "And you're not going to do that, are you?"

"I'd still remember," said the child.

His father smiled. "Would you?"

"I'd remember Patricia." He pressed the guinea pig hard to his small chest. "And what's more," he said triumphantly, "I'd remember her in English!"

Everyone laughed. Richard got up and said they must leave, but before they could do so there was a noise on the landing and a girl of about nine appeared, lugging a large impassive baby in her arms.

"He wants his supper," she announced, and a slightly younger girl following behind her shouted, "And so do I!" They both dissolved into giggles and Anna found herself being introduced to them while at the same time saying her farewells to their parents. In the confusion the baby was dumped on the floor with the guinea pig until Elizabeth picked it up again and it began with great concentration to suck the end of her sleeve.

James saw Anna and Richard to the door. "Best of luck," he said through the children's shouted goodbyes. "And think about what I said."

Anna was left with the picture of Elizabeth standing at the top of the stairs and smiling with the baby in her arms.

"I told you she was nice," said Richard as they started on their walk back.

She nodded. The rain had stopped but it must have lasted some time, for the pavements were sodden.

"I wonder if I could really write something of my own," she said. "It'd be interesting to try. If I do have to go to Mama, I don't suppose I'd have to be away very long."

"Probably just a few days."

Notting Hill Gate was deserted. The demonstrators, no doubt discouraged by the downpour, had all gone home. A torn placard lying in a puddle was the only sign that they had ever been there.

"You know what I really hate about going to Berlin?" said Anna, picking her way round it. "I know it's stupid, but I'm frightened the Russians might suddenly close in and take it over and then I'd be trapped. They couldn't. could they?"

He shook his head. "It would mean war with America."

"I know. But it still frightens me."

"Were you very frightened when you escaped from Germany?"

"That's what so silly. I never realized till much later what it had been about. In fact, I remember making some idiotic remark at the frontier and Mama having to shut me up. Mama made it all seem quite normal." They trudged along among the puddles. "I wish at least I'd answered her letter," she said.

Once back in the flat, she became very practical. "We'd better make a list," she said, "Of all the things that have to be seen to, like the rug being delivered. And what are you going to eat while I'm away? I could cook something tonight for you to warm up."

She made the list and decided about the food, and by the time Konrad's call was due she felt ready to cope with anything he might say. Sitting by the telephone, she rehearsed the various things she wanted to ask him and waited. He came through punctually at nine o'clock. There was a jumble of German voices and then his, reassuringly calm.

"How is Mama?" she asked.

"Her condition is unchanged," he said and then in what was obviously a prepared speech, "I think it is right that you should come tomorrow. I think that one of her relatives should be here."

"Of course," she said. She told him the number of her flight and he said that he would meet it.

Richard, listening beside her, said, "What about Max? Has he told him?"

"Oh yes," she said. "What about Max?"

Konrad said that he had not yet cabled Max – that must mean that there was no immediate danger, thought Anna – but that he would do so if necessary in the morning. Then he said in his concerned refugee voice, "My dear, I hope you're not too upset by this. I'm sorry to have to break up the family. With luck it won't be for long."

She had forgotten that he always referred to Richard and herself as the family. It was friendly and comforting and she suddenly felt much better.

"That's all right," she said. "Richard sends his love." There was something more she wanted to ask him, but she had trouble remembering what it was. "Oh yes," she said. "How did Mama ever develop pneumonia in the first place?"

There was a silence, so that at first she thought he had not heard. Then his voice answered, and even through the distortion of long distance she could tell that it sounded quite different.

"I'm sorry," he said flatly. "But your mother took an overdose of sleeping pills."

Sunday

Anna's feet were so heavy that she could only walk very slowly. It was hot in the street and there was no one about. Suddenly Mama hurried past. She was wearing her blue hat with the veil, and she called to Anna, "I can't stop – I'm playing bridge with the Americans." Then she disappeared into a house which Anna had not even noticed. She felt sad to be left alone in the street like that, and the air was getting hotter and heavier all the time.

It shouldn't be so hot so early in the morning, she thought. She knew it was early because Max was still asleep. He had taken the front wall off his house to let out the heat, and she could see him sitting in his living-room with his eyes closed. Beside him his wife Wendy was blinking drowsily in a chair with the baby in her arms. She looked at Anna and moved her lips, but the air had become too thick to carry the sound and Anna could not hear her, so she walked away, along the hot, empty street, with the hot, empty day stretching before her.

How did I come to be so alone? she thought. Surely there must be someone to whom I belong? But she could think of no one. The heavy air pressed in on her, so that she could hardly breathe. She had to push it away with her hands. And yet there *was* someone, she thought, I'm sure there was. She tried to remember his name, but her mind was empty. She could think of nothing, neither his name nor his face nor even his voice.

I must remember, she thought. She knew that he existed, hidden in some tiny wrinkle of her brain, and that without him nothing was any good, nothing would ever be any good again. But the air was too heavy. It was piled up all round her, pushing in on her chest, even against her eyes and her nose and her mouth. Soon it would be too late even to remember.

"There *was* someone!" she shouted, somehow forcing her voice through the thickness. "I know there was someone!"

And then she was in bed with the sheets and blankets twisted all round her and a pillow half over her face, and Richard saying, "It's all right, love. It's all right."

For a moment she could only lie there, feeling him close and letting the horror flow out of her. She half-saw, half-felt the familiar room, the shapes of a chair, a chest of drawers, the faint glint of a mirror in the darkness.

"I had a dream," she said at last.

"I know. You nearly blew me out of bed."

"It was that awful one when I can't remember you."

His arms were round her. "I'm here."

"I know."

In the glow from the street lamp outside the window, she could just see his face, tired and concerned.

"It's such an awful dream," she said. "Why do you suppose I have it? It's like being caught in some awful shift of time and not being able to get back."

"Maybe some trick of the brain. You know – one lobe remembering and the other not picking it up till a fraction of a second later. Like déjà vu, only the other way round."

It did not comfort her.

"Suppose one got stuck."

"You couldn't get stuck."

"But if I did. If I really couldn't remember you. Or if I got stuck even earlier, before I'd learned to speak English. We wouldn't even be able to talk to each other."

"Yes, well," he said, "in that case we'd have other problems as well. You'd be about eleven years old."

At this she laughed and the dream, already fading, receded into harmlessness. She could feel herself aching from lack of sleep and remembered clearly, for the first time, about the previous day.

"Oh God," she said. "Mama."

His arms tightened about her. "I suppose all this worry has stirred up things you'd almost forgotten. About losing people – people and places – when you were small."

"Poor Mama. She was awfully good then, you know."

"I know."

"I wish to God I'd written to her." Through the gap between the curtains the sky looked black. "What time is it?"

"Only six o'clock." She could see him peering at her anxiously in the darkness. "I'm sure it would have made no difference whether you'd written or not. There must have been quite other reasons. She must have been worried about something, or terribly upset."

"D'you think so?" She wanted to believe him.

"And then, maybe, she thought of your father – how he had died – and she thought, why shouldn't she do the same?"

No, it wasn't right.

"Papa was different," she said. "He was old, and he'd had two strokes. Whereas Mama . . . Oh God," she said, "I suppose some people have parents who die naturally." She stared into the darkness. "The trouble is, you see, I don't suppose Max has written either, or if he did, the letter may not have got there from Greece."

"It still wouldn't be a reason to commit suicide."

Outside in the street there was a clinking of bottles followed by a clip-clop of the milkman's horse as it walked on to the next house. A car started up in the distance.

"We were all so close, you see, all those years," she said. "We couldn't help it, moving from country to country with everything against us. Mama used to say, if it weren't for Max and me, it wouldn't be worth going on – and she did get us through, she kept the family together."

"I know."

"I wish I'd written to her," she said.

Richard came with her on the bus to the airport. They said goodbye in the echoing lounge which smelled of paint and she left him, calmly, as she had planned.

But then, quite suddenly, as she pulled out her passport ready for inspection, despair swept over her. To her horror, she found tears pouring down her face, soaking her cheeks, her neck and even the collar of her blouse. She could not move but only stood there blindly, waiting for him to catch up with her.

"What is it?" he cried, but she didn't know either.

"I'm all right," she said. "I really am." She was horrified at having frightened him so. "It's not having slept," she said. "And I'm getting the curse. You know I always weep when I'm getting the curse."

Her voice came out quite loud, and a man in a bowler hat turned and looked at her in surprise.

"I could still come with you," said Richard. "I could get a flight later today or tomorrow."

"No, no, of course not. I'm really all right." She kissed him. Then she took her passport and ran. "I'll write to you," she shouted back to him.

She knew it was stupid, but she felt that she was leaving him for ever.

Once on the plane, she felt better.

She had only flown twice before and still found it exciting to look down on a world of toy-sized fields and houses and tiny, crawling cars. It was a relief to be out of it all and to know that Berlin was still some hours away. She looked out of the window and thought only of what she could see. Then halfway across the North Sea, clouds appeared, and soon there was only a blanket of grey below and bright, empty sky above. She leaned back in her seat and thought about Mama.

It was curious, she thought. Whichever way one imagined Mama, it was always in movement: the blue eyes frowning, the lips talking, Mama clenching her hands with impatience, tugging her dress into place, dabbing violently at her tiny snub nose with a powder puff. She did not trust anything connected with herself to function properly unless she kept tabs on it, and even then she always felt it could be improved.

Anna remembered how, during one of her visits from Germany, Mama had once brought Konrad round to her digs for lunch. Anna had cooked the only dish she knew, which was a large quantity of rice mixed with whatever happened to be on hand. On this occasion the ingredients had included some chopped-up sausages, and Konrad had said, politely, how nice they were. At once Mama had said, "I'll find you some more," and to Anna's irritation she had snatched up the bowl and rootled through it, to toss a succession of small sausage pieces on to his plate.

How could anybody so obsessed with the minutiae of every day suddenly want to stop living? Not that Mama hadn't often talked about it. But that was in the last years in Putney when she and Papa had been so utterly wretched, and even then it had not seemed like anything to be taken seriously. Her cries of "I wish I was dead!" and "Why should I go on?" had been so frequent that both Anna and Papa had soon learned to ignore them.

And the moment things improved, the moment the endless worry about money was lifted from her, her enthusiasm for life had returned – both Anna and Papa had been surprised how quickly. She had written long excited letters home from Germany. She had gone everywhere and looked at everything. She had translated so well for the Americans in the Control Commission that she had soon been promoted – from Frankfurt to Munich, from Munich to Nuremberg. She had wangled lifts home on American troop planes to arrive with presents for everyone – American whisky for Papa, nylon stockings for Anna, real silk ties for Max. And she had been thrilled when at last the British Control Commission had decided that Papa, too, should make an official trip to Germany.

Hamburg, thought Anna. Did the flight to Berlin pass over it? She peered down at the flat country which showed every so often through gaps in the cloud. It was strange to think that somewhere down there might be the place where Papa lay buried. If Mama died, she supposed she'd be buried with him. If Mama dies, she thought suddenly with a kind of impatience, I'll be the child of two suicides.

There was a click as something was put down on the folding table in front of her, and she became aware of the stewardess standing nearby.

"I thought you might like some coffee," she said.

Anna drank it gratefully.

"I was so sorry to hear of the illness in your family," said the girl in her American voice. "I do hope that when you get to Berlin you will find everything better than you expected."

Anna thanked her and stared out at the brilliant sky and the melting clouds below. But what do I expect? she thought. Konrad had only told her that Mama's condition was unchanged, not what that condition was. And in any case, that had been last night. By now . . . No, thought Anna, she's not dead. I would know if she were.

As the time of arrival approached, she tried to think what it would be like meeting Konrad. One thing, it wouldn't be difficult to find him, because he was so tall and fat. She'd see him over the heads of the other people. He'd be leaning on his walking stick if his back was giving him trouble as it so often did, and he'd smile at her with his curiously irregular features and say something reassuring. He would be calm. Anna imagined him always having been calm. You'd have to be calm to stay on in Germany under Hitler as a Jewish lawyer defending other Jews, as he had done.

He had even remained calm when they sent him to a concentration camp. By being calm and unobtrusive, he had survived several weeks, until his friends managed to get him out. Nothing too terrible had happened to him, but he would never talk about what he had seen. All he would say was, "You should have seen me when I came out," and he would slap his paunch and grin his lopsided grin and say, "I was thin – like a Greek youth."

He would certainly have made sure that Mama had the best possible treatment. He was very practical. Anna remembered Mama telling her that in England he had supported a wife and two daughters by taking a job in a factory. The daughters were grown up now, but he seemed not to care too much for any of them and seldom went home.

"We are now approaching Tempelhof airfield," said the stewardess, and all the lighted messages about seat belts and cigarettes flicked on.

She looked out of the window. They were still quite high and the airport was not in sight. I suppose all this is still East Germany, she thought, looking down at the fields and little houses. They looked like anywhere else and presumably would have looked just the same under the Nazis. I only hope we land in the right place, she thought.

The last time she had landed in Berlin had been with Richard. They had arrived at short notice, to tell Mama that they were getting married. It had been a curious, edgy visit, even though she'd been so happy – partly because she so hated being in Berlin and only partly because of Mama. Not that Mama had been against the marriage – on the contrary, she had been delighted. Only Anna had known that for years Mama had secretly dreamed of her marrying someone quite different.

In Putney, when Papa's health was failing and everything seemed hopeless, Mama had had a kind of running fantasy about this marriage. It would be to a lord – a very grand kind of lord with a big estate in the country. Anna would live with him at the castle, and Mama would live at the dower house (there always was a dower house, she had explained to Anna). There would be an apple-cheeked housekeeper to cook muffins for Mama to eat in front of the fire, and on fine days Mama would ride about the grounds on a white horse.

Of course she hadn't meant it. It had just been a joke to cheer them both up and, as Anna had frequently pointed out, Mama couldn't ride. Even so, when she told Mama about Richard, she knew that somewhere in her mind Mama was regretfully relinquishing the image of herself prancing about on this great bleached beast, surrounded by grooms or hounds or whatever she'd imagined for herself, and it had made Anna nervous.

Another thing that had made her nervous was that Mama did not really understand Richard's work. She got most of her information about England from Max who, as a rising young barrister, seemed to her a more reliable source than Anna with her art, and Max had told her that he did not have a television set, though they were considering buying one for the au pair girl. This had made Anna nervous of what Mama might say to Richard, or even when Richard was anywhere near, because Mama's voice was so loud.

It was silly because Richard was quite able to take care of himself. But she had been grateful to Konrad for steering Mama away from dangerous subjects. As soon as Mama got started on literature or drama (she tended, in any case, only to quote Papa's views, and not always correctly) he had looked at her with his nice, ugly smile and said, "It's no use talking about these things in my presence. You know perfectly well that I'm illiterate."

The plane tilted to one side. Anna could see Berlin, suddenly close, above the wing, and the airport beyond it. We'll be down in a minute, she thought, and all at once she felt frightened.

What would Konrad tell her? Would he blame her for not having written to Mama for so long?

Did he even know why Mama had taken the overdose? And how would she find Mama? Conscious? In an oxygen tent? In a coma?

As the ground came towards her, it was like the first time she'd jumped off the high diving board at school. I'm going into it, she thought. Nothing can stop it now. She saw with regret that there was not even a veil of cloud to delay her. The sky was clear, the midday sun blazed down on the grass and tarmac of the airport as it rushed up towards her, then the wheels touched, they roared briefly along the runway and stopped with a shudder. There was nothing to be done. She was there.

Konrad was standing near the door of the arrival lounge, leaning on his walking stick as she had expected. She walked towards him through the blur of German voices, and when he caught sight of her he came to meet her.

"Hullo," he said, and she saw that his large face looked worn out and somehow skimpy. He did not embrace her, as he normally did, but only smiled at her formally and shook her hand. She was at once apprehensive.

"How is Mama?" she asked.

He said, "Exactly the same." Then he told her flatly that Mama was in a coma and had been ever since she had been found on Saturday morning and that there had been some difficulty in treating her because for a long time no one knew what she had taken. "I cabled Max this morning," he said.

She said, "Shall we go to the hospital?"

He shook his head. "There's no point, I've just come from there."

Then he turned and walked towards his car, slightly ahead of her, in spite of his bad back and his walking stick, as though he wanted to get away from her. She hurried after him in the sunshine, more and more distressed.

"What do the doctors say?" she asked, just to make him look round, and he said wearily, "The same. They simply can't tell," and walked on.

It was all much worse than anything she had imagined. She had thought he might blame her for not having written to Mama, but not to the extent of wanting nothing to do with her. She was appalled at the thought of coping with all the horrors to come alone, without his support. (If only Richard were here, she thought, but cut the thought off quickly, since it was no use.)

When he reached the car, she caught up with him and faced him before he could put the key in the lock.

"It was because of me, wasn't it?" she said. "Because I hadn't written?"

He lowered the hand with the key in it and looked back at her, utterly astonished.

"It would certainly be a good idea if you wrote to your mother more often," he said, "and if your brother did too. But that is not the reason why she tried to kill herself."

"Then why?"

There was a pause. He looked away from her,

over her right shoulder, as though he had suddenly seen someone he knew in the distance. Then he said stiffly, "She had grounds to believe that I was no longer faithful to her."

Her first reaction was, impossible, he's making it up. He was saying it to comfort her, so that she shouldn't blame herself if Mama died. For heaven's sake, she thought, at their age! Well, she supposed that if she had ever thought about it, she would have assumed that Mama's relationship with him had not been entirely platonic. But this!

Very carefully, she said, "Are you in love with someone else?"

He gave a sort of snort of "No!" and then said in the same stiff voice as before, "I had an affair."

"An affair?"

"It was nothing." He was almost shouting with impatience. "A girl in my office. Nothing."

She tried to think of a reply to this but couldn't. She felt completely out of her depth and climbed into the car in silence.

"You'll want some lunch."

He seemed so relieved to have got the bit about the affair off his chest that she thought it must really be true.

As he started the car, he said, "I want to make your stay here as pleasant as possible. In the circumstances. I know it's what your mother would wish. If possible even like a little holiday. I know you didn't get away in the summer."

For God's sake, she thought.

He made a gesture of impatience. "I understand, of course, that you'd give anything not to be here but at home with Richard. I only meant that when you're not at the hospital – and at the moment there is not much you can do there – you should have as pleasant a time as can be arranged."

He glanced at her from behind the steering wheel and she nodded, since he seemed so anxious for her to agree.

"Well," he said, "we may as well start by going somewhere pleasant for lunch."

The restaurant was set among the pine trees of the Grunewald, a popular place for family outings, and on this fine Sunday it was packed. Some people were even drinking at small tables outside, their overcoats well-buttoned against the chilly air.

"Do you remember this place?" he asked.

She had already had a faint sense of recognition – something about the shape of the building, the colour of the stone.

"I think I may have come here sometimes with my parents. Not to eat, just for a drink."

He smiled. "*Himbeersaft.*"

"That's right." Raspberry juice, of course. That's what German children always drank.

Inside, the dining-room was steaming up with the breath of many good eaters, their coats hung in rows against the brown panelled walls, and mounted above them, two pairs of antlers and a picture of a hunter with a gun. Their voices were loud and comfortable above the clinking of their knives and forks, and Anna found herself both moved and yet suspicious as always, at the sound of the Berlin accents so familiar from her childhood.

"This thing with your mother has been going on for nearly three weeks," said Konrad in English, and the voices with their complicated associations faded into the background. "That's how long she had known."

"How did she find out?"

"I told her."

Why? she thought, and as though he had heard her, he went on, "We live in a very narrow circle. I was afraid she might hear from someone else."

"But if you don't really love this woman – if it's all over?"

He shrugged his shoulders. "You know what your mother is like. She said that things could never again be right between us. She said she'd had to start again too many times in her life, she'd had enough, that you and Max were grown up and no longer needed her –" He waved his hand to indicate all the other things Mama had said and which Anna could only too easily imagine. "She's been talking about killing herself for nearly three weeks."

But he hadn't actually said that it was all over between himself and the other woman.

"The affair, of course, is finished," he said.

When the food arrived, he said, "We'll go to

the hospital after lunch. Then you can see your mother and perhaps talk to one of the doctors. In the meantime, tell me about yourself and Richard."

She told him about Richard's serial, about the flat and about her new job.

"Does this mean that you'll eventually become a writer?"

"Like Richard, you mean?"

"Or like your father."

"I don't know."

"Why don't you know?" he asked almost impatiently.

She tried to explain. "I don't know if I'd be good enough. Till now I've really only tinkered with other people's plays. I've never done anything of my own."

"I could imagine you being a good writer."But he added at once, "Of course I know nothing about it."

They tried to talk about general subjects: Hungary, but neither of them had listened to the radio that morning, so they did not know the latest news; the German economic recovery; how long it would take Max to get a flight from Greece. But gradually the conversation faltered and died. The sound of the Berliners eating and talking seeped into the silence. Familiar, long forgotten words and phrases.

"*Bitte ein Nusstörtchen*," a fat man at the next table told the waiter.

That's what I always used to eat when I was

small, she thought. A little white iced cake with a nut on top. And Max had always chosen a *Mohrenkopf*, which was covered in chocolate and had cream inside. They had never wavered in their preferences and had both come to believe that the one was only for the girls and the other for boys.

"*Ein Nusstötchen*," said the waiter and set it down in front of the fat man.

Even now, for a fraction of a second, Anna was surprised that he let him have it.

"You're not eating," said Konrad.

"I'm sorry." She speared a bit of potato on her fork.

"Try to eat. It'll be better. The next few days are bound to be difficult."

She nodded and ate while he watched her.

"The hospital your mother is at is German. It's just as good as the American for this kind of case, and it was nearer. Also I thought that if your mother recovered, it would be easier for her if the Americans didn't know about her suicide attempt." He waited for her to agree, and she nodded again. "When I found her –"

"You found her?"

"Of course." He seemed surprised. "You understand, I've been afraid of this happening. I stayed with her as much as possible. But the night before, she seemed all right, so I left her. Only next day I had such a feeling . . . I went round to her flat and there she was. I stood and looked at her and didn't know what to do."

"How do you mean?"

"Perhaps . . ." he said, "perhaps it was really what she wanted. She'd said again and again that she was tired. I don't know — I still don't know if what I did was right. But I thought of you and Max, and I felt I couldn't take the responsibility."

When she could eat no more, he stood up.

"Come along," he said. "We'll go and see your mother. Try not to let it distress you too much."

The hospital was a pleasant, old-fashioned building set in a wooded park. But even as they approached the front door, past a man raking leaves and another shovelling them into a wheelbarrow, her stomach tightened on the lunch she had not wished to eat, so that for a moment she was afraid she might be sick.

Inside the hall, a very clean nurse in a starched apron received them. She had a tight expression and seemed to disapprove of them both, as though she blamed them for what had happened to Mama.

"Follow me please," she said in German.

They went, Anna first with Konrad behind her. It was more like a nursing home than a hospital — wood panelled walls and carpets instead of tiles and lino. It's more like a nursing home than a hospital, she said to herself, so as not to think about what she was going to see. Corridors, stairs, more corridors, then a large landing crowded with cupboards and hospital equipment. Suddenly the nurse stopped and pointed, and there, behind a piece of dust-sheeted machinery, was a bed. There was someone in it, motionless. Why was Mama not in her room? Why had they put her here, on this landing?

"What's happened?" she shouted so loudly that she frightened all three of them.

"It's all right," said Konrad, and the nurse explained in disapproving tones that nothing had happened: since Mama had to be under constant observation, this was the best place for her. Doctors and nurses crossed the landing every few minutes and were able to keep an eye on her.

"She's being very well looked after," said Konrad, and they went over to the bed and looked at Mama.

You could not see very much of her. Just her face and one arm. All the rest was covered with bedclothes. The face was very pale. The eyes were closed – not just closed normally but closed tight, as though Mama were keeping them shut on purpose. There was something sticking out of her mouth, and Anna saw that it was the end of a tube through which Mama's breath came thinly and irregularly. Another tube led to the arm from a bottle suspended from a stand near the bed.

"There doesn't seem to be any change," said Konrad.

"It is necessary to bring her out of the coma," said the nurse. "For this we must call her by her name." She leaned over the bed and did so. Nothing at all happened. She shrugged her shoulders. "*Na*," she said, "a familiar voice is always better. Perhaps if you speak to her she will hear."

Anna looked down at Mama and the tubes.

"In English or in German?" she asked, and immediately wondered how she could have said anything so stupid.

"That you must decide for yourself," said the nurse. She nodded stiffly and disappeared among the dustsheeted equipment.

Anna looked at Konrad.

"Try," he said. "One doesn't know. It may do some good." He stood looking at Mama for a moment. "I'll wait for you downstairs."

Anna was left alone with Mama. It seemed quite mad to try and talk to her.

"Mama," she said tentatively in English. "It's me, Anna."

There was no response. Mama just lay there with the tube in her mouth and her eyes tightly shut.

"Mama," she said more loudly. "Mama!"

She felt oddly self-conscious. As though that mattered at a time like this, she told herself guiltily.

"Mama! You must wake up, Mama!"

But Mama remained unmoving, her eyes obstinately closed and her mind determined to have nothing to do with the world.

"Mama!" she cried. "Mama! Please wake up!"

Mama, she thought, I hate it when your eyes are shut. You're a naughty Mama. Clambering on Mama's bed, Mama's big face on the pillow, trying to prise the eyelids open with her tiny fingers. For God's sake, she thought, that must have been when I was about two.

"Mama! Wake up, Mama!"

A nurse carrying some sheets came up behind her and said in German, "That's right." She smiled as though she were encouraging Anna in some kind of sport. "Even if there is no reaction," she said, "your voice may be getting through."

So Anna went on shouting while the nurse put the sheets into a cupboard and went away again. She shouted in English and in German. She told Mama that she must not die, that her children needed her, that Konrad loved her and that everything would be all right. And while she was shouting, she wondered if any of it were true and whether it was right to tell Mama these things even when she probably could not hear them.

In between shouting, she looked at Mama and remembered her in the past. Mama tugging at a sweater and saying, "Don't you think it's nice?" Mama in the flat in Paris, triumphant because she'd bought some strawberries at half-price. Mama beating off some boys who had pursued Anna home from the village school in Switzerland. Mama eating, Mama laughing, Mama counting her money and saying, "We'll have to manage somehow." And all the time a tiny part of herself observed the scene, noted the resemblance to something out of Dr Kildare, and marvelled that anything so shattering could also be so corny.

At last she could bear it no longer and found the nurse who led her back to Konrad.

She felt sick again in the car and hardly saw the hotel where Konrad had booked her in. There was an impression of shabbiness, someone leading her up some stairs, Konrad saying, "I'll fetch you for supper," and then she was lying on a large bed under a large German quilt in a strange, half-darkened room.

Gradually, in the quiet, the sick feeling receded. Tension, she thought. All her life she had reacted like this. Even when she was tiny and afraid of thunderstorms. She had lain in bed, fighting the nausea among the frightening rumbles and flashes of lightning, until Max got her a freshly-ironed handkerchief from the drawer to spread on her stomach. For some reason this had always cured her.

They had slept under German quilts like this one, not sheets and blankets as in England. The quilts had been covered in cotton cases which buttoned at one end and, to avert some long forgotten, imaginary misfortune, they had always shouted, "Buttons to the bottom!" before they went to sleep. Much later, in the Hamburg hotel after Papa's death, she had reminded Max of this, but he had not been able to remember anything about it.

That had been the last time they had all been together, she and Max and Mama and Papa – even though Papa was dead. For Papa had left so many notes and messages that for a while it had felt as though he were still with them.

"I *told* him not to," Mama had said, as though it were a case of Papa going out without his galoshes on a wet day. She had not wanted Papa to write any farewell notes because suicide was still a crime, and she did not know what would happen if people found out. "As though it were anyone's business but his own," she said.

She had left Papa one evening, knowing that after she had gone he would take the pills she had procured for him, and that she would never again see him alive. What had they said to each other that last evening? And Papa – what would he think of all this now? He had wanted so much for Mama to be happy. "You are not to feel like a widow," he had written in his last note to her. And to Max and herself he had said, "Look after Mama."

There was a shimmer of light as a draught shifted the curtains. They were made of heavy, woven cloth, and as they moved, the tiny pattern of the weave flowed and changed into different combinations of verticals and horizontals. She followed them with her eyes, while vague, disconnected images floated through her mind: Papa in Paris, on the balcony of the poky furnished flat where they had lived for two years, saying, "You can see the Arc de Triomphe, the Trocadero and the Eiffel Tower!" Meeting Papa in the street on her way home from school. London? No, Paris, the Rue Lauriston where later, during the war, the Germans had had their Gestapo headquarters.

Papa's lips moving, oblivious of passers-by, shaping words and phrases, and smiling suddenly at the sight of her.

The boarding house in Bloomsbury on a hot, sunny day. Finding Mama and Papa on a tin roof outside an open window, Papa on a straight-backed chair, Mama spread out on an old rug. "We're sunbathing," said Papa with his gentle, ironic smile, but specks of London soot were drifting down from the sky, blackening everything they touched. "One can't even sunbathe any more," said Mama, and the bits of soot settled on Mama and Papa and made little black marks on their clothes, their hands and their faces. They got mixed up with the pattern on the curtains, and still Mama and Papa sat there with the soot drifting down, and Anna too was drifting – drifting and falling. "The most important thing about writing," said Richard, but the plane was landing and the engines made too much noise for her to hear what was so important, and Papa was coming to meet her along the runway. "Papa," she said aloud, and found herself in the strange bed, unsure for a moment whether she had been asleep or not.

At any rate it could only have been for a minute, for the light had not changed. It's Sunday afternoon, she thought. I'm in a strange room in Berlin and it's Sunday afternoon. The draught moved the curtains again, and little patches of light danced over the quilt, across the wall, and disappeared. It must still be sunny outside. She got up to look.

Outside the window was a garden with trees and bushes and fallen leaves in the long grass. Near the dilapidated wooden fence something moved, flashing orange, leapt, clung to a wildly dipping branch, scrabbled the right way up and sat swinging in the wind. A red squirrel. Of course. There were plenty of them in Germany. She watched it as it sat washing itself, with the wind ruffling its tail. She no longer felt sick at all.

Papa would have liked the swinging squirrel. He had never known about Richard, or about Max's baby daughter, or that the world, after years of horror and deprivation, had once again turned into such a delightful place. But I'm alive, she thought. Whatever happens, I am still alive.

Konrad came to collect her at six o'clock. "We're spending the evening with friends," he said. "I thought it would be best. They'd originally invited your mother and myself for bridge, so they were expecting me anyway. Of course they only know that she has pneumonia."

Anna nodded.

As they drove through the darkened, leafy streets, she was filled again with the sense of something half-familiar. Yellow lights flickered through the trees, casting wavering shadows on the ground.

"This is all the Grunewald district," said Konrad. "Where you used to live. Do you remember any of it?"

She did not remember the streets, only the feel of them. She and Max walking home after dark, playing a game of jumping on each other's shadows as they slid and leapt between one street lamp and the next. Herself thinking, this is the best game we've ever played. We'll play it always, always, always . . .

"It was hardly touched by the bombing," said Konrad. "Tomorrow you might like to have a look round near your old home."

She nodded.

A group of shops, unexpectedly bright, throwing rectangles of light on to the pavement. *Apotheke*, a chemist. A newsagent. A florist. *Blumenladen* said the illuminated sign above it, and as she read the word she had a sensation of being suddenly very near the ground, surrounded by great leaves and overpowering scents. Enormous brilliant flowers nodded and dipped above her on stems almost as thick as her wrist, and she was clutching a huge hand from which a huge arm stretched up into the jungle above her. *Blumenladen*, she thought softly to herself. *Blumenladen*. Then the shop vanished into the darkness and she was back in the car, a little dazed, with Konrad beside her.

"Nearly there," he said in English, and after a moment she nodded again.

He turned down a side street, through a patch of trees, and stopped outside a white-painted building, one of a number placed fairly close together among scrappy lawns.

"Purpose-built American flats," he said. "The Goldblatts have only just moved in here."

They climbed a flight of stairs and as soon as Hildy Goldblatt opened the door Anna felt she was back in wartime England, for with her frizzy hair, her worried dark eyes and her voice which sounded as though someone had sat on it, she seemed like the epitome of all the refugees she had ever known.

"There she is," cried Hildy, opening her arms wide. "Come all the way from London to see her sick Mama. And how is she today?"

Konrad replied quickly that Mama's pneumonia was fractionally better – which was true, he had telephoned the hospital before leaving – and Hildy nodded.

"She will be well soon."

Her husband, a slight man with grey hair, had appeared in the hall beside her. "Today pneumonia is nothing. Not like in the old days."

"In the old days – *na ja*." They raised their hands and their eyebrows and smiled at each other, remembering not only the intractability of pneumonia but all the other difficulties overcome in the past. "Things are different today," they said.

As Hildy led the way to a lavishly laid table ("We eat now," she said, "then it will be done,") Anna wondered how they had preserved their refugee accents through all the years in England and of working with the Americans in Germany. It must be a special talent, she decided. She could almost have predicted the meal Hildy served, as well. In wartime London it would have been soup with knoedel, followed by apple tart. In Berlin, with the American PX to draw on, there was an additional course of steak and fried potatoes.

While Hildy heaped her plate ("So eat – you must be tired!") the conversation slid from English into German and back again in a way which she found curiously soothing. Erwin Goldblatt worked with Konrad at J.R.S.O., the Jewish Restitution Successor Organization, where they dealt with claims from the millions of Jews who had lost their families, their health and their possessions under the Nazis. "Of course you can't really compensate them," said Erwin. "Not with money." And Konrad said, "One does what one can." They talked of work, of the old days in London ("I can tell you, Finchley in 1940 was no summer holiday!"), of colleagues in Nuremberg where they had all first met.

"And your brother?" asked Hildy. "What is he doing? Something in Greece, your mother said."

"He's got a big case for a Greek ship owner," said Anna. "He had to go there for a conference, and the ship owner lent him a house for a holiday with his family afterwards. The trouble is, it's so far away even from Athens, on a tiny island. It's bound to take him a long time to get here."

Hildy looked surprised. "Max too is coming to see his mother? Is it then so serious?"

I shouldn't have said that, thought Anna.

Konrad swept in calmly. "Pneumonia is no

joke, even today, Hildy. I thought it best to let him know."

"Of course, of course." But she had guessed something. Her shrewd eyes met her husband's briefly, then moved back to Konrad. "So much trouble," she said vaguely.

"Ach, always trouble." Erwin sighed and offered Anna some cake. "But this young man," he said, brightening, "such a young barrister, and already ship owners are lending him their country houses. He is making quite a career."

"You've heard her talk about him," cried Hildy. "The wonder boy. He got a big scholarship in Cambridge."

"And a law scholarship after that," said Anna.

Hildy patted her hand. "There, you see," she said, "it will be all right. As soon as the mother sees her son, no matter how ill she is, she will just get up from her bed and walk."

Everyone laughed, and it was quite true, thought Anna, Mama would do anything for Max. At the same time another part of herself thought, then what in heaven's name am I doing here? But she suppressed it quickly.

Hildy went into the kitchen and reappeared a moment later with a jug of coffee. "The girl looks tired," she said, passing Anna her cup. "What can we do for her?"

Erwin said, "A glass of cognac," but Hildy shook her head. "Cognac afterwards. First I know something better."

She beckoned, and Anna followed her out of the

room, feeling suddenly at the end of her tether. I don't want any cognac, she thought, and I don't want any more cake or coffee, I just want to be home. She found herself standing beside Hildy in the hall. There was nothing there except a telephone on a small table. Hildy pointed to it.

"So why don't you ring up your husband?" she asked.

"Really?" said Anna. She felt tears pricking her eyes and thought, this is really ridiculous.

"Of course."

"Well, if you're sure." She blinked to stop the tears from running down her face. "I don't know what it is – I feel so –" She couldn't think what it was she felt like.

Hildy patted the telephone.

"Ring him up," she said and left Anna alone in the hall.

When she went back into the living-room, they were all drinking cognac.

"Look at her," cried Erwin when he saw her, "she has another face already."

Konrad patted her shoulder. "Everything all right?"

"Yes." Just hearing Richard's voice had made her feel different.

Out of respect for Hildy's telephone bill, they had only spoken a few minutes. She had told him that she had seen Mama – but nothing about Konrad, it would have been impossible with him in the next room – and he had told her that he was trying to get on with the script and that he had cooked himself some spaghetti.

Halfway through she had suddenly asked, "Am I speaking with a German accent?" but he had laughed and said, "Of course not." Afterwards she had felt reconnected to some essential part of herself – something that might, otherwise, have come dangerously loose.

"I'm sorry," she said. "It's all been a bit disorientating."

They gave her some cognac which she drank, and suddenly the evening became very cheerful. Erwin told various old refugee jokes which Anna had known since her childhood but which, for some reason, she now found hilarious. She saw that Konrad, too, was leaning back, laughing, in his chair.

"Ach, the troubles we've had, the troubles we've had." Hildy had produced another cake, a chocolate one, and was pressing it on everyone. "And in the end, somehow, it's all right, and you think, all that worrying – better I should have spent the time learning another language."

Everyone laughed at the thought of Hildy attempting another language on top of her refugee English, and she pretended to threaten them with the chocolate cake.

"You can laugh," she said, "but all the same it's true what I say. Most things are all right in the end." She glanced at Erwin. "Not everything, of course. But most things."

Erwin looked back at her fondly. "*Na*," he

said, "at least they're better than they used to be."

When Anna got back to her hotel room she felt almost guilty at having enjoyed the evening so much. But what else could I have done? she thought. Lying under the German quilt in the darkness, she could hear a cat wailing in the garden. Somewhere in the distance a train went chuntering across some points.

She suddenly remembered that when she was small, too, she had listened to distant trains in bed. Probably it's the same line, she thought. Sometimes when she had found herself awake while everyone else was asleep, she had been comforted by the sound of a goods train rumbling interminably through the night. After Hitler, of course, goods trains had carried quite different cargoes to quite different destinations. She wondered if other German children had still been comforted by their sound in the night, not knowing what was inside them. She wondered what had happened to the trains afterwards, and if they were still in use.

The cat wailed and the chugging of another train drifted over on the wind. Perhaps tomorrow Mama will be better, she thought, and fell asleep.

Monday

When she woke up in the morning, it was pouring. She could hear the rain drumming on the window and dripping from the gutters even before she opened her eyes on the grey light of the room. In the garden, most of the leaves had been washed off the trees, and she hoped that the cat had found some shelter.

As she made her way downstairs, across worn carpets and past ancient, fading wallpapers, she noticed for the first time that what she was staying in was not a real hotel, but a private house, half-heartedly converted. There did not seem to be many other guests, for the breakfast room was empty except for an elderly man who got up and left as she arrived. She sat down at the only other table which had been laid, and at once a small bow-legged woman whom she dimly remembered from the previous day hurried in with a tray.

"Had a good sleep?" she asked in broad Berlinese. "You're looking better today. When I saw you yesterday I thought to myself, that one's had all she can take."

"I'm fine now, thank you," said Anna. As usual, she emphasized her English accent and spoke more haltingly than necessary. She had no wish to be thought even remotely German.

"I'll bring you your breakfast."

The woman was middle-aged, with pale hair so lacking in colour that it might have been either fair or grey, and sharp, pale eyes. As she scuttled in and out on her little legs, she talked without stopping.

"The gentleman phoned to say that he'd be calling for you at nine. It's dreadfully wet out. String rain, we call it in Berlin, because it looks like long pieces of string, d'you see? I really dread going out to do the shopping, but I have to, there's no one else to do it."

As she talked, she brought Anna a small metal can of tea, butter, jam and bread rolls.

"Thank you," said Anna, and poured herself some tea.

"I don't do suppers, but I can always fix you up a boiled egg or some herrings if you should want them. Or a bit of cauliflower."

Anna nodded and smiled in a limited way, and the woman, defeated by her English reserve, retired.

She looked at her watch. It was only a little after eight-thirty, she had plenty of time. She wondered how Mama was. Presumably the same, otherwise Konrad would have asked to speak to her when he rang. She buttered one of the bread rolls and took a bite. It tasted much as she remembered from her childhood.

"There are more rolls if you'd like them," said the woman, peering round the door.

"No thank you," said Anna.

When she was small, there had never been more than one roll each for breakfast. "If you want more, you can eat bread," Heimpi who looked after them always told them while she and Max wolfed it down before school. She had been so convinced of the infallibility of this rule that once, pondering upon the existence of God and also feeling rather hungry, she had challenged Him to a miracle.

"Let them give me a second roll," she had told Him, "then I'll know that You exist," and to her awed amazement Heimpi had actually produced one.

It had been a poor bargain, she thought. For months afterwards she had been burdened by the knowledge that she alone in a family of agnostics had proof of God's existence. Though she found it exciting at first (standing talking to Mama and Papa, her hands secretly folded in prayer behind her back, thinking, "Little do they know what I'm doing!"), eventually it had become such a strain that Mama had asked her if she were worried about anything. She remembered looking at Mama in the sunlight from the living-room window, trying to decide what to answer.

As always in those days, she was worried not only about God but about several other things as well, the most urgent being a book of raffle tickets she had recklessly acquired at school and had found impossible to sell. Should she tell Mama about the raffle tickets or about God? She had carefully examined Mama's face – the directness of her blue eyes, the childish snub nose and the energetic, uncomplicated mouth, and she had made her decision. She had told her about the raffle tickets.

As she sat chewing her roll in the shabby breakfast room, she wished she had told her about God instead. If it had been Papa, of course she would have done.

"I'm going now," said the woman. She had put on a long, shapeless coat which concealed her legs, and was carrying an umbrella. On her head was a hat with a battered veil.

"*Auf Wiedersehen*," she said.

"*Auf Wiedersehen*," said Anna.

For a moment she had a glimpse of Mama in a hat with a veil. The veil was blue, it just reached the end of Mama's nose, and it was crumpled because Mama was crying. When on earth was that? she wondered, but she could not remember.

Konrad arrived punctually, shaking the water from his hat and coat.

"Your mother's pneumonia is a little better," he said. "Otherwise she's much the same. But I managed to speak to the doctor when I rang, and he said they were trying a different treatment."

"I see." She did not know whether that was good or bad.

"Anyway, he'll be at the hospital, so you can speak to him yourself. Oh, and Max rang up from Athens. He's hoping to get on a flight to Paris this afternoon, in which case he'll be here either tonight or tomorrow."

"Oh good." The thought of Max was cheering.

"He only knows about the pneumonia, of course."

"Not about the overdose?"

"He didn't ask me, so I didn't tell him," said Konrad stiffly.

Watching him drive through the pouring rain, she noticed again how worn he looked. There were dark circles under his eyes, and not only his face but even his large body looked a little collapsed. Of course, he's been coping with all this far longer than me, she thought. But as they approached the hospital, her stomach tightened as it had done the previous day at the prospect of seeing Mama, and she felt suddenly angry. If Konrad hadn't had an affair with some wretched typist, she thought, none of this would have happened.

Unlike the previous day, the reception hall was full of bustle. Nurses hurried to and fro, the telephone kept ringing while a man in a raincoat stood dripping patiently at the desk, and immediately behind them an old lady in a wheelchair was being manoeuvred in from the rain under several black umbrellas. Of course, she thought, this was Monday. Yesterday most of the staff would have had the day off.

The nurse behind the desk announced their arrival on the telephone and a few minutes later a slight, balding man in a white coat came hurrying towards them. He introduced himself as Mama's doctor with a heel-clicking little bow and plunged at once into an analysis of Mama's condition.

"Well now," he said, "the pneumonia no longer worries me too much. We've been pumping her full of antibiotics and she's responded quite well. But that's no use unless we can bring her out of the coma. We've made no progress there at all, so we've given her some powerful stimulants in the hope that these may help. You'll find her very restless."

"Restless?" said Anna. It sounded like an improvement.

He shook his head. "I'm afraid the restlessness does not mean that she's better. It's just a reaction to the drugs. But we're hoping that it will lead to an improvement eventually."

"I see," she said. "What –?" She was suddenly unsure how to put it in German – "What do you think is going to happen?"

He spread-eagled the fingers of both hands and showed them to her. "Fifty-fifty," he said in English. "You understand? If she comes out of the coma – no problem. She'll be well in a few days. If not . . ." He shrugged his shoulders. "We're doing all we can," he said.

At first, when she saw Mama, in spite of what the doctor had told her, she thought for a moment that she must be better. From the far side of the landing, with Mama's bed partly obscured by a large piece of hospital equipment, she could see the bedclothes move as though Mama were tugging at them. But there was a nurse standing by the bed, doing something to Mama's arm, and as she came closer she saw that it had been bandaged on to a kind of splint, presumably to stop Mama dislodging the tube which led to it from the bottle suspended above the bed.

Tethered only by her arm, Mama was lurching violently about in the bed, and every so often a strange, deep sound came from her chest, like air escaping from an accordion. She no longer had the tube in her mouth, but her eyes were tightly shut, and she looked distressed, like someone in a nightmare, trying to escape.

"Mama," said Anna, gently touching her face, but Mama suddenly lurched towards her, so that her head almost struck Anna's chin, and she drew back, alarmed. She glanced at Konrad for comfort, but he was just staring down at the bed with no expression at all.

"It's the drugs," said the nurse. "The stimulants acting on the barbiturates she's taken. It causes violent irritation."

Mama flung herself over to the other side, dislodging most of the bedclothes and exposing a stretch of pink nightdress. Anna covered her up again.

"Is there nothing you can give her?" she asked the nurse. "She looks so – she must be feeling terrible."

"A sedative, you mean," said the nurse. "But she's had too many of those already. That's why she's here."

Mama moved again and her breath came out in a kind of roar.

The nurse gave the bandaged arm a final pat where it was connected to the tube. "In any case," she said quite kindly, "your mother is unconscious. She is not aware of anything that is happening."

She nodded to Konrad and went.

Anna looked at Mama and tried to believe what the nurse had said, but Mama did not look unaware of what was happening. Apart from the fact that her eyes were closed, she looked, as she had so often looked in the past, as though she were railing at something. Death, or being kept alive. There was no way of telling which.

She hoped that perhaps Konrad would try to speak to her, but he just stood there leaning on his stick, with a closed face.

Suddenly Mama gave a tremendous lurch, her legs kicked the bedclothes right off and she fell back on to the bed with one of her strange moans. Her pink nightie which Anna remembered her buying during her last visit to London was rucked up round her waist, and she lay there, shamefully exposed on the rumpled sheets.

Anna jumped to tug down her nightdress with one hand, while trying to replace the bedclothes with the other. The nurse, reappearing from somewhere, helped her.

"Look at those legs," she said, patting Mama's thigh as though she owned it. "Marvellous skin for her age."

Anna could not speak.

Once, in the Putney boarding house, Mama had rushed into their joint bedroom in great distress. It seemed she had been sitting in the lounge, her legs outstretched towards the meagre fire, trying to get warm, and a dreadful, crabby old man sitting opposite had suddenly pointed to somewhere in the region of his navel and said, "I can see right up to here." Mama had been particularly upset because the old man was one of the few English residents, which seemed to make it much worse than if he had just been a refugee. "It was horrible," she had cried and had collapsed on the bed to burst into tears. Anna had been filled with rage at the old man, but, while she comforted Mama with a kind of fierce affection, she had also wished quite desperately that Mama had just sat with her knees together like everyone else, so that none of it could have happened.

Now, as Mama threw herself about and they all stood looking down at her, she felt the same mixture of rage and tearing pity. She tried to tuck in a sheet, but it became dislodged again almost at once.

"I really think there is no point in your staying here at the moment," said the nurse. "Come back this afternoon, when she'll be calmer."

Konrad touched her arm to guide her away from the bed. She pulled away from him, but she could see that what the nurse had said was true, and after a moment she followed him across the landing. Her last glimpse of Mama was of her face, eyes closed, the mouth emitting a wordless shout, as it rose into view behind some shrouded piece of equipment and then fell back again out of sight.

The reception hall was full of people in wet coats, and the smell of steaming cloth made her feel sick again. It was still pouring: you could see the water streaming down the windows. Konrad stopped near the door, where a little fat woman stood peering out, waiting for a break in the downpour.

"Look, I'm sorry," he said, "but I have to go to my office." His voice sounded hoarse and unused, and she realized that he had hardly spoken since they had arrived at the hospital. "There's a meeting this morning, and everybody would think it very odd if I didn't turn up."

"It doesn't matter," she said. "I can look after myself."

"Don't be silly. I'm not going to leave you here in this weather. I can just imagine what your mother would think of that."

The little fat woman flung herself out into the

rain, shooting her umbrella open at the same time, and disappeared down the steps. A cold breath of wet air reached Anna before the door closed behind her and she breathed it gratefully.

"I thought if I could find you an occupation for this morning, we could meet for lunch. There's been a small exhibition here in memory of your father – your mother must have written to you about it."

"Is there?" She did not want to see any exhibition, least of all one that would remind her of Papa.

He looked at her. "You're feeling awful."

"I think I'd just as soon go back to the hotel. Perhaps when Max comes tomorrow –"

"Of course." He glanced at his watch. "I'll drive you back."

Her coat was not particularly waterproof, and even the short distance to the car was enough almost to soak her. He looked at his watch again as she sat dripping on to the upholstery.

"You'll never get dry in that hotel. The woman probably turns the heating down during the day. It's a miserable place, but it was all I could find. Everywhere else was full."

She shook her head. "It really doesn't matter."

"Well, I don't want two invalids on my hands." He started the car. "I'll take you to my flat. At least I know it's warm there."

As they drove through the downpour, water blurred the windscreen in spite of the wipers, and she could hear it beating on the roof of the car above the sound of the engine. Every so often she caught a glimpse of streaming pavements, dripping awnings, bent figures running under shiny umbrellas. Konrad sat leaning forward over the steering wheel, trying to see the road ahead.

"What time is your meeting?" she asked.

He glanced down at his watch. "Five minutes ago. They'll just have to wait."

His flat was in a side street like that of the Goldblatts, and as he stopped the car outside it, water from a huge puddle in the gutter shot over the curb and over the feet of an old man who shouted something and shook his umbrella at him. He insisted on holding the car door open for her, standing in the rain with water dripping from his hat, and then they both hurried across the pavement into the dry.

"I'll be all right now," she said as soon as he had ushered her into his hall, but he stayed, fussing over a hanger for her coat, telling her to make herself some coffee, and checking that the radiators were turned up.

"Till lunch, then," he said, and then hesitated in the doorway. "By the way," he said, "you will find a number of feminine possessions lying about. They are of course all your mother's."

"Of course," she said, astonished. It would not have occurred to her to think anything else.

"Yes, well –" He waved awkwardly. "See you later."

For a moment after the door had shut behind him, she stood in the dark little hall, wondering what to do. Then a trickle of water ran down her neck and she went into the bathroom to rub her wet hair with a towel.

As in the Goldblatts' flat, everything was very new and modern. There was a shower, a big mirror and a bath mat with flowers printed on it. On the shelf above the basin were two blue tooth mugs, each with a tooth-brush in it. She supposed that one of them belonged to Mama.

Konrad had put some instant coffee and biscuits ready for her in the kitchen, and she was just pouring hot water into the cup, when she was startled by the ringing of the telephone. At first she could not remember where the telephone was. Then she found it in the far corner of the living-room. She ran over to it, picked up the receiver and discovered that her mouth was full of biscuit. Swallowing frantically, she could hear a German voice at the other end ask with rising insistence, "Konrad? Konrad, are you all right? Are you all right, Konrad?"

"Hullo," she said through a mouthful of crumbs.

"Hullo." The voice – a woman's – sounded put out. "Who is that, please?"

She explained.

"Oh, I see." The voice became very business-like. "This is Dr Rabin's secretary speaking. Could you tell me what time Dr Rabin left his flat, please? Only he is rather late for a meeting at his office."

Anna told her.

"Oh, thank you, then he will soon be here."

There was a little pause, then the voice said, "I am sorry to have troubled you, but you understand, his colleagues were getting rather worried."

"Of course," said Anna, and the voice rang off.

She went back to her coffee in the kitchen and drank it slowly. That must have been her, she thought. The girl in his office. She had sounded quite young. Somehow, it had not occurred to her that she would still be there, working with him. It seemed to make everything more uncertain. Poor Mama, she thought. But another part of her examined the situation in terms of plot and thought angrily, how corny.

When she had finished her coffee, she wandered round the flat. It was tidy, well furnished and impersonal. The curtains in the living-room were almost exactly the same as the Goldblatts' – obviously it was all American Army issue. There was a bookshelf with a few paperbacks, nearly all detective stories, and a desk with a framed snapshot of a middle-aged woman and two girls in their twenties – his wife and daughters she supposed. The woman was wearing a flowered dress with a home-made look. Her hair was swept back neatly into a bun and she had a sensible, faintly self-satisfied expression. A real German *Hausfrau*, thought Anna.

The bedroom was not quite as tidy as the living-room. Konrad must have had a bit of a rush getting up. The cupboard door was slightly open and inside it she could see one of Mama's dresses among his suits. Her pale blue bathrobe hung beside his on the door and her hair brush lay on his dressing table. Next to it and half-surrounded by the cord of his electric shaver was a small glass dish in which nestled some of Mama's beads, a safety pin and half a dozen hairgrips.

She picked up the beads and ran them through her fingers. They were iridescent blue glass – Mama loved them and wore them all the time. Then she suddenly thought, but she doesn't use hairgrips. Mama's hair was short and curly. There was nothing to grip. Unless of course she had been washing her hair and had wanted to pin it in a particular way. That must be it, she thought. The fact that she had never seen Mama do this did not mean that it never happened. The hairgrips must be hers.

All the same, as she went back into the living-room, she felt suddenly very much alone. It occurred to her that she really knew very little about Konrad. After all, he had presumably abandoned his wife for Mama. Might he not be ready now to abandon Mama for someone else? And what would Mama do then, even if she got better? She relied on him so much, not only for his love but for his help. After years of trying to cope alone with the family's practical problems (and though Mama was more practical than Papa, thought Anna, she was still unpractical by most people's standards) she had found it almost incredible that Konrad should be prepared to look after her.

"He is so good to me," she had once told Anna.

Anna had waited to hear in what way and Mama, too, had evidently found it difficult to describe. "Do you know," she had said at last with a kind of awe, "he can even wrap parcels."

It was still raining, though not nearly so hard. Outside the window, across the road, she could see the wet roofs of other American blocks of flats, one of them Mama's.

She wondered what Mama had thought about when she took the barbiturates. She wondered if she had looked out of her window, if it had been wet or fine, if it had been dusk or already dark. She wondered if she had not had any regrets for the sky and the street lamps and the shadowed pavements and the sound of the passing cars. Clearly she must have felt that without Konrad they were not worth having. But perhaps she had not thought at all. Perhaps she had just been angry and had swallowed the pills, thinking, that will show him. Unlike Papa, she had left no notes for anyone.

There was some writing paper on Konrad's desk, and she spent the rest of the morning writing to Richard. It was a relief to be able to tell him everything that had happened, from Konrad's affair to her own reactions. When she had finished the letter she felt better. She stuck it down, put on her coat which had completely dried out on the radiator, slammed the front door as Konrad had told her, and went to meet him for lunch.

Probably because of the hairgrips and the telephone call, she felt uneasy as soon as she saw him. What shall I say to him? she thought. He was waiting for her in a small restaurant off the *Kurfürsten Damm*, newly rebuilt against a background of ruins still awaiting demolition. He rose at once to greet her.

"You found it," he said. "I'd have come to pick you up in the car, but the meeting went on and on. And as the rain had stopped –"

"It was no trouble," she said.

"I rang the hospital before I came out, and they think you should go and see your mother some time after four. They think she'll be in a better state by then."

"All right."

"I can get away before five. I could drive you there."

"There's no need," she said. "I'll make my own way."

There was an awkward little silence, then he said, "Anyway, you got dry."

"Yes, thank you."

"Good news today about Hungary. Have you seen it?"

She shook her head.

"They've told the Russians to get out."

"Really?"

"Yes." He produced a folded newspaper from his coat pocket, but was suddenly hailed by a small man with rabbity teeth who had appeared at their side.

"My dear Konrad," cried the little man, "I was hoping to see you."

"Hullo, Ken," said Konrad.

Was he pleased or annoyed at the interruption? It was impossible to tell. He introduced him, politely as usual, as Ken Hathaway from the British Council.

"Looking after the poetry side," said Mr Hathaway, smiling through his teeth and looking disconcertingly like Bugs Bunny. He pointed to the paper. "Isn't that amazing?" he cried. "Just told them to leave. Scram. Skedaddle. Vamoose. Back to Mother Russia. Mind you, I'm not surprised. Very fiery people, the Hungarians."

"Do you think the Russians will really go?"

Konrad shrugged his shoulders. "It would be a very remarkable thing if they did."

Mr Hathaway appeared to have sat down at their table, and after a moment – it must be because he, too, was finding it difficult to be alone with her, thought Anna – Konrad asked him to join them for lunch.

"I was so very sorry to hear of your mother's illness," said Mr Hathaway, and Konrad produced his usual vague phrases about pneumonia. Mr Hathaway managed somehow to make his teeth droop in sympathy. "Do give her my love," he said. "I admire her so much." He turned to Anna. "She has such enthusiasm, such a feeling for life – for living it to the full. I always think that's a very continental quality."

Anna agreed a little sadly about Mama's enthusiasm for life, thinking at the same time how cross it would make her to hear herself described as continental. There was nothing Mama was quite as proud of as her British citizenship. She always referred to herself and the British as "we" (whereas Anna would go to infinite trouble to circumvent such phrases) and had once even talked, in her slight but unmistakable German accent, about "when we won the First World War," to everyone's confusion.

"And her feeling for the arts," cried Mr Hathaway. "Her love of the theatre – I suppose that must have been nurtured by your father. But her music was her very own. To me, she stands for a very special kind of flowering, a special European –" He suddenly ran out of words and said, "Anyway, we're all very fond of her here," with such genuine feeling that Anna decided he was really quite nice, in spite of his teeth and his foolishness.

It was odd, she thought, but she had quite forgotten about Mama's music. When she was small, the sound of the piano had seemed as much part of Mama as the way she looked. Every day while Papa wrote in his study, Mama had played and even composed. She'd been good, too, people said. But with the emigration, it had all stopped. If she had continued, would she have had something to hang on to in the present crisis instead of swallowing a bottleful of pills? And had she stopped because of the endless, crushing worries, or had the music never, really, been essential to her – only part of the romantic image she had of herself? There was no way of knowing.

"We'll miss her on Wednesday," said Ken

Hathaway, and it transpired that he was giving a party to which both Mama and Konrad had been invited. "Perhaps you would consider coming in her place?" He smiled hopefully over a forkful of schnitzel.

"Oh, I couldn't possibly," said Anna.

She was appalled at even thinking about Wednesday. Suppose Mama was still in a coma by then? Suppose she was worse? Then she saw Mr Hathaway's face and realized how rude she must have sounded.

"I mean," she said, "it must depend on how my mother is."

"Let's say I'll bring her if her mother can spare her," said Konrad, making everything normal again.

She knew that he was doing it for Mama's sake, to make life easier for her if she recovered, but it still worried her that he should be so good at covering up.

"Was there something you wanted to talk to me about?" he asked Ken Hathaway, who at once launched into an account of a poetry reading he had arranged, at which he hoped as many people as possible would turn up.

By Wednesday Mama may be dead, thought Anna.

A small German boy at the next table was eating cherry cake, and his mother was nagging him not to swallow the stones.

"What happens to people who swallow cherry stones?" he asked.

"What happens to people when they die?" Anna had once asked Mama in German, long ago when she was still a German child.

"Nobody knows," Mama had said. "But perhaps when you grow up, you'll be the first person to find out," and after that she had been less frightened of death.

She must have eaten without noticing, for suddenly Konrad was paying the bill.

"Can I drive you anywhere?" he asked. "It's still too early to go to the hospital. What would you like to do?"

"I thought perhaps I'd just walk about."

"Walk about?"

"Where we used to live. It's the only bit I remember."

"Of course."

He dropped her off where she asked him, having first provided her with a street map, as well as detailed instructions for getting to the hospital and then back to her hotel.

"I'll ring you after six," he said. "Look after yourself."

She waved and watched him drive off.

It was not the first time she had been back to this part of Berlin. Two years before, she had walked here with Richard and Mama. She had pointed out to Richard all the places she remembered, and Mama had explained various changes which had happened since. They had chatted all the way – it had been a lovely day, she remembered – and she had been so happy that Richard and Mama were getting on so well that she had little time for any other emotions. Now, as she stood alone in the gusty wind, it felt quite different.

Konrad had dropped her at the end of the street where she had lived as a child. How ordinary it looked. She had to check the nameplate at the corner to make sure it was the right one.

When she was small, the street had always seemed to her very dark. The pavements were lined with trees planted at short intervals, and when Mama and Papa had told her that they were going to live there instead of their old flat in a perfectly good light street with no trees at all, she had thought, they're mad, and had wondered dispassionately whatever foolishness they would get up to next. That had been in the summer – she must have been four or five – when the leaves had made a kind of awning right across the road. Now most of the leaves were on the ground, swept into piles in the gutter, and the wind blew through bare branches.

She had expected the house to be quite a long way down, but she reached it almost at once. It was hardly recognizable – she knew it wouldn't be from her previous visit. Instead of their small family villa, it had been extended into a building containing three expensive looking flats. The gabled roof had been flattened and even the windows looked different.

Only the garden still sloped down to the fence as it had done in the past, and so did the little paved drive where Max had taught her to ride his bicycle. ("Isn't there an easier way to learn?" she had asked him when, unable to brake or reach the ground with her feet, she had repeatedly crashed into the gate at the bottom. But he had told her there wasn't, and she had believed him as always.)

Then she noticed that something else was unchanged. The steps leading up to the front door – now the entrance to one of the flats – were exactly as she remembered them. The steepness, the colour of the stone, the slightly crumbly surface of the balustrade, even the rhododendron bush wedged against its side – all this was exactly as it had been more than twenty years before.

She stared at it, remembering how, after school, she had raced up there, pulling at the bell, and, as soon as the door was opened, shouting, "Is Mama home?"

For a moment, as she looked at it, she remembered exactly what it had felt like to do this. It was as though, for a fraction of a second, she had half-seen, half-become the small, fierce, vulnerable person she had once been, with her lace-up boots and socks held up by elastic bands, her fear of volcanoes and of dying in the night, her belief that rust caused blood poisoning, liquorice was made of horses' blood, and there would never be another war, and her unshakeable conviction that there was no problem in the world that Mama could not easily solve.

The small person did not say, "Is Mama home?" She said, "*Ist Mami da?*" and did not speak a word of English, and for a moment Anna felt shaken by her sudden emergence.

She walked a few steps along the fence and tried to peer round the side of the house. There had been some currant bushes there once, and beyond them – she thought she could still see the beginning of it – a kind of wooden stairway leading to the terrace outside the dining-room.

In the hot weather she, or the small person she had once been, had sat on that terrace to draw. She had had a round tin filled with crayons of different lengths, old pencil shavings and other odds and ends, and when you opened it, these had emitted a particular, delightful smell.

Once, during her religious period, she had decided to sacrifice one of her drawings to God. First she had thought of tearing it up, but then that had seemed a pity – after all, for all she knew, God might not even want it. So she had closed her eyes and thrown it up into the air, saying – in German, of course – "Here you are, God. This is for You." After allowing plenty of time for God to help himself, if He were so minded, she had opened her eyes again to find the drawing on the floor, and had put it calmly back into her drawing book.

Afterwards – or it might have been some other time altogether – she had walked through the French windows into the dining-room, to find Mama standing there in a big white hat. As her eyes adjusted to the indoor darkness and the colours returned to the curtains, the tablecloth

and the pictures on the walls, she had thought
how beautiful it all was, especially Mama. She
had looked at Mama's face in surprise because
she had never thought about her in that way
before.

Beyond the terrace, out of sight at the back of
the house, was the rest of the garden, probably
neatly planted now, but in those days a grassless
waste which Mama had sensibly handed over to
Max and herself. There they had played football
(herself in goal, vague about where the goalposts
were supposed to be, uninterested in stopping the
ball), they had wrestled and built snowmen and
dug holes in the ground, hoping to reach the centre
of the earth.

Once in the summer she had sat in the shade
of the pear tree with Heimpi and had watched
her embroider new eyes on her favourite stuffed
Pink Rabbit in place of the glass ones which
had fallen out.

When they had fled from the Nazis, Pink
Rabbit had been left behind, embroidered eyes
and all, with all their other possessions, and so
had Heimpi whom they could no longer afford
to pay. She wondered what had happened to
them both.

The wind sang in the branches above her
head and she walked on, past the place where
she used to retrieve her tortoise as it tried to
escape from the garden, past the place where
a man had exposed himself to her on a bicycle
("On a bicycle?" Papa had said in amazement,

but Mama had said – she could not remember what Mama had said, but whatever it was, it had made it all right, and she had not been worried about it).

At the corner of the street, where she and Max's gang had always met to play after school, she stopped in surprise.

"Wo ist denn die Sandkiste?"

She was not sure whether it was she who had said it or the small person in boots who seemed, suddenly, very close. The sandbox, containing municipal sand to be scattered on snowy roads in winter, had been the centre of all their games. It had marked the dividing line between cops and robbers, the starting point of hide-and-seek, the place where the net would have been when they played tennis with a rubber ball and home-made wooden bats. How could anyone have taken it away? She and the small person in boots could not get over it.

But the rowan trees were still there. *Vogelbeeren*, they were called in German, and once Mama, seeing the red berries ripening, had cried regretfully, "Already." When Anna had asked her why, Mama had said that it meant the end of summer.

A car passed, trailing petrol fumes, and the street seemed suddenly empty and dull. She walked back slowly towards the main road.

There was the paper shop where she had bought her drawing books and crayons, her exercise books and the special blue paper with which they had to be covered. She had gone inside it with Mama on her previous visit, but it was under different management and no one had remembered her. The greengrocer next door had gone, but the kiosk at the old tram stop was still there and still sold burnt sugared almonds in tiny cardboard boxes, even though there were no more trams, only buses.

Next came the café and, round the corner, the general shop, still two steps down from the pavement, where Heimpi had sometimes sent her on errands. *Bitte ein Brot von gestern*. Why had Heimpi always insisted on yesterday's bread? Perhaps because it was easier to cut. The numbers of the trams were 76, 176 and 78. There was something unreliable about the 78, it did not always stop long enough. Once, as it passed him Max had put his gym shoes on the step – *Turnschuhe*, they were called – and had not got them back for two days.

Hagen Platz. Fontane Strasse. Königsallee.

This was where she had turned off to go to school. She had walked with her best friend Marianne who was older and could draw ears front view. *"Quatsch!"* she had shouted when they had disagreed, and Marianne had called her *ein blödes Schaf*, which was a silly sheep.

A flurry of leaves – *Herbstblätter* – blew along the pavement, and she felt suddenly disorientated. What am I doing here? she thought in German. *Was tue ich eigentlich hier? Die Mami wartet doch auf mich*. But where was Mama waiting? At home, beyond the door at the top of the worn stone steps, waiting to hear what had happened at school today? Or groaning and struggling under the covers of her hospital bed?

Something seemed about to overwhelm her. The clouds, piled huge and grey in the sky, seemed to press down on her head. (*Die Wolken*, she thought in slow motion, as in a dream.) The pavement and the leaves rose treacherously under her feet. There was a wall behind her. She leaned against it. Surely I'm never going to faint, she thought. And then, out of the shifting sky, an unmistakable voice addressed her.

"My dear, you look as pale as cheese," it said, and a face surrounded by frizzy hair blocked out the rest of the world. She recognized the kindness before she remembered the name. Hildy Goldblatt, from the previous night. Of course, she thought, they live near here. A hand supported her arm. Another slipped round her shoulder. Then pavements and trees were swimming past and Hildy's voice, like God's, came out of nowhere. "What you need is a cup of tea," she said. "Not, of course that they can make it properly here." There was a sudden rush of warmth with the opening of a door, and then Anna found herself settled behind a table in the café with some hot tea before her.

"Now then," said Hildy, "I hope you're feeling better."

She drank the tea and nodded.

Had she once sat at this table, eating cakes with Mama? But the whole place, flooded in yellow neon light, had changed too much for her to remember.

"I'm sorry," she said. "It's all been a bit overwhelming."

"Of course." Hildy patted her hand. "And worrying about your poor Mama. Mothers worrying about their children, that's nothing, they're used to it. But the other way round is always bad." There was some cake on a plate before her and Anna watched her put some in her mouth. "Are you going to the hospital later?"

"Just for a moment." She was afraid that Hildy would want to come with her, but Hildy only nodded.

"Good," she said. "You will have your tea, and perhaps a cake – No? Are you sure? – And I will try not to talk like a chatterbox as Erwin always tells me, and then, when you are feeling better, I will put you in a taxi. All right?"

Anna nodded gratefully.

Behind Hildy, through the café window, she could see the pavement of the *Königsallee*. She and Max had passed that way each day on their way to school. Funny, she thought, you'd think it would have left some kind of a mark. All those times. On their own . . . with Mama and Papa . . . with Heimpi . . .

The waitress hovered. Hildy filled up her cup. "*Ach ja, bitte noch ein Stückchen Kuchen,*" and there was another piece of cake, apple this time, and Hildy was eating it.

"I saw your mother only two weeks ago," said

Hildy. "She showed me some pictures of her summer holidays," and suddenly they were at the seaside, she was quite small and Mama's face was above her, huge and smiling against the summer sky.

"*Mami, Mami, Mami!*" she squealed.

There was sand between her toes, and her woollen bathing suit clung to her wet legs and to her sandy body where Mama was holding her.

"*Hoch, Mami! Hoch!*"

She flew up into the sky. The sea was like a great wall at the end of the beach, and Mama's face, suddenly beneath her, laughed up from the shining sand.

"She always enjoys everything so much," said Hildy.

"Yes," said Anna.

She could still see Mama, the brilliant blue eyes, the open, laughing mouth, and the blazing beach behind her. Like a vision, she thought. And then it faded, and there was Hildy at the other side of the table, looking concerned.

"I don't want Mama to die," she said childishly, as though Hildy could arrange it.

"Well, of course you don't." Hildy refilled her cup and stirred more sugar into it. "Drink," she said.

Anna drank.

"I think your mother won't die," said Hildy. "After all, however it may seem just now, she still has very much to live for."

"Do you think so?" The hot, sweet tea had warmed her and she was beginning to feel better.

"Of course. She has two nice children, a grand-child already, perhaps more to come. She has a job and a flat and friends."

Anna nodded. "It's just – she had a bad time for so many years."

"Listen!" Hildy peered at her across the tea-cups. "My Erwin worked at Nuremberg. I know what happened to the Jews who stayed behind. *They* had a bad time." And as Anna looked at her in surprise, "When you've finished your tea, you go to the hospital, and I hope your mother – I hope the pneumonia will be not so bad. And if she can hear you, you tell her it's time she got better."

"All right." For the first time she found herself laughing, because Hildy made it all sound so simple.

"That's right." Hildy finished the last crumbs on her plate. "People," she said, without explaining exactly whom she meant by them, "people shouldn't give up so easy."

At the hospital she was received by the nurse who had been on duty that morning. "Your mother is calmer now," she said in German, and led Anna up the familiar corridors and stairs. For a moment, after her vision of Mama on the beach, it was surprising to see her grey-haired and middle-aged. She was lying quietly under the covers, her breathing almost normal, so that she might have been asleep. Only once in a while her head turned restlessly on the pillow and the untethered hand twitched.

Anna sat down on the bed and looked at her. She's fifty-six, she thought. Mama's eyes were tightly closed. There were deep frown lines between them, and two further lines ran to the pulled-down corners of her mouth. The chin had lost some of its firmness, it was pudgy now rather than round. The hair straggled on the pillow. But in the middle of it all was the nose, tiny, snub and incongruously childish, sticking up hopefully from the ageing face.

When I was small, thought Anna, I used to have a nose like that. Everyone had told her that her nose was just like Mama's. But then, some time during her adolescence, her nose had grown and now – though it certainly wasn't a Jewish nose, Mama had said – it was straight and of normal length. Somehow Anna always felt that she had grown up past Mama along with her nose. Hers was a more serious nose, an adult nose, a nose with a sense of reality. Anyone with a nose like Mama's, she thought, was bound to need looking after.

Mama stirred. The head came a little way off the pillow and dropped back again, the closed eyes facing towards her.

"Mama," said Anna. "Hullo, Mama."

Something like a sigh escaped from the mouth, and for a moment she imagined that it had been in reply to her voice, but then Mama turned her head the other way and she realized that she had been mistaken.

She put her hand on Mama's bare shoulder, and Mama must have felt that, for she twitched away very slightly.

"Mama," she said again.

Mama lay motionless and unresponsive.

She was about to call her again when, deep inside Mama, a sound began to form. It seemed to rise up slowly through her chest and her throat and finally emerged roughly and indistinctly from her half-open lips.

"*Ich will*," said Mama. "*Ich will*."

She knew at once what it was that Mama wanted to do. Mama wanted to die.

"*Du darfst nicht!*" she shouted. She would not allow it. She was so determined not to allow it that it took her a moment to realize that Mama had actually spoken. She stared down at her, amazed and with a kind of anger. Mama tried to turn her head away, and the strange sound rose up in her again.

"*Ich will*," she said.

"*Nein!*"

Why should she remember, now of all times, about the pencil sharpener that Mama had stolen from Harrods? It was a double one in a little pig-skin case, and Mama had given it to her for her fourteenth or fifteenth birthday. She had known at once, of course, that Mama could not possibly have paid for it. "You might have been caught," she had cried. "They might have sent for the police." But Mama had said, "I just wanted you to have it."

How could anyone be so hopelessly, so helplessly wrong-headed, stealing pencil sharpeners and now wanting to die?

"Mama, we need you!" (Was it remotely true? It didn't seem to matter.) "You must not die! Mama!" Her eyes and cheeks were wet and she thought, bloody Dr Kildare. "*Du darfst nicht sterben! Ich will es nicht! Du musst zurück kommen!*"

Nothing. The face twitched a little, that was all.

"*Mami!*" she shouted. "*Mami! Mami! Mami!*"

Then Mama made a little sound in her throat. It was absurd to imagine that there could be any expression in the toneless voice that came from inside her, but to Anna it sounded matter of fact, like someone deciding to get on with a job that needed to be done.

"*Ja, gut,*" said Mama.

Then she sighed and turned her face away.

She left the landing in a state of confused elation. It was all right. Mama was going to live. Your little brother will play the violin again, she thought, and felt surprised again at the corniness of it all.

"I spoke to my mother and she answered me," she told the nurse. "She's going to get better."

The nurse pursed her lips and talked about the Herr Doktor's opinion, but Anna did not care. She knew she was right.

Even Konrad was cautious.

"It's obviously an improvement," he said on the telephone. "I expect we'll know more tomorrow."

He had heard from Hildy Goldblatt about her moment of faintness in the *Königsallee* and was anxious to know if she were all right. "I'll come and pick you up for supper," he said, but she did not want to see him and told him that she was too tired.

Instead, she ate scrambled eggs served on a not-very-clean tablecloth in the deserted breakfast room and thought about Mama.

The bow-legged proprietress hovered nearby and talked – about the Nazis (she had never been one, she said), about the concentration camps of which she had known nothing, and about the bad times just after the War. No food, she said, and such dreadfully hard work. Even the women had to clear the rubble.

Her Berliner voice, a bit like Heimpi's, like all the voices of Anna's childhood, went on and on, and, even though Anna believed little of what she said, she did not want it to stop. She answered her in German and was surprised to find that when she really tried, she could speak it almost perfectly.

"Is' doch schön, dass es der Frau Mutter 'n bischen besser geht," said the woman.

Anna, too, was glad that Mama was a little better.

"Sehr schön," she said.

Tuesday

Tuesday began with a telephone call from Konrad. Anna was still in bed, when she was wakened by the knocking at her door, and she had to run down to the telephone in the hall with her coat thrown over her nightdress, the crumbly lino chilling her bare feet as she said, "Hello? Hello, Konrad?"

"My dear," Konrad's voice sounded much more positive, "I'm sorry I woke you. But I thought you'd like to know straightaway that I've just spoken to the doctor, and he says your mother is going to be all right."

"Oh, I'm so glad." Even though she had been sure of it, she was surprised by the wave of relief which flooded over her. "I'm so glad!"

"Yes – well – so am I." He gave a little laugh. "As you can imagine."

"Yes."

"Well, I just thought I'd tell you. So you could

have your breakfast in peace. I'll meet you at the hospital at nine-thirty."

"All right." It felt like an outing, a party, a celebration. "And thanks, Konrad. Thanks for letting me know."

She hurried back to her room to put on her clothes, and had hardly got them on before she was called to the telephone again. This time it was Max, from the airport.

"Max," she cried, "it's all right. Mama is going to be all right."

"I know." He sounded in control of the situation, as always. "I've just spoken to the hospital."

"Did they tell you –?"

"The overdose. Yes." There was a pause. "It's funny," he said. "I've been sitting in planes and at airports for two days with nothing to do but think about Mama, but that possibility never occurred to me. I just kept wondering whether she'd be alive when I got here."

"I know." She could hear his breathing through the telephone – fast, shallow breaths. He must be dead tired.

"Do you know why she did it?"

"Konrad," she said. "He had an affair."

"Konrad? Good God." He was as amazed as she had been. "I thought it was something to do with us. I hadn't written for a bit."

"I know. I hadn't either."

"Good God," he said again, and then became very practical. "Look, I don't know what sort of transport I can get from here, but I'll get to the hospital as soon as I can. You meet me there."

"All right." The odd feeling of it being a celebration returned to her as she said, "See you then."

"See you then," he said and rang off.

She rushed through her breakfast with only the briefest replies to the proprietress who was determined to continue the conversation of the previous night. Even so, when she arrived at the hospital, Max was already there. He was talking to the nurse behind the desk and she recognized not only his back, but also the expression on the nurse's face – that special smile, denoting pleasure and eagerness to help, which he had been able to induce in almost everyone he met since he had been about seventeen.

"Max," she said.

He turned and came towards her, looking tired but unrumpled in his formal suit, and most of the visitors and patients looked up to watch him.

"Hello, little man," he said, and in answer to the old endearment, left from their joint childhood, she felt a glow spread through her, and smiled back at him much as the nurse had done. "What a lot of trouble," he said as he kissed her, "Bringing up our poor Mama."

She nodded and smiled. "Have you spoken to Konrad?"

"Just for a moment. He gave me your number. He said something about taking full responsibility. I couldn't think what he meant."

"He feels very badly about it."

"Well, so he should. Though perhaps . . . Mama isn't easy." Max sighed. "Oh, I don't know. Has he said anything about what he's going to do?"

"Not exactly. But he said the affair meant nothing to him – that it's all finished."

"I suppose that's something."

"Yes."

There was a pause. She was conscious of the other people and the nurse behind the desk watching them. "He's coming here at nine-thirty," he said. "Do you want to wait for him or go and see Mama first?"

"Let's go and see Mama," he said, and she thought how much easier it would be to face going up to the landing now that Mama was better, and with Max beside her.

As they started along the corridor which smelt of disinfectant and polish as usual, she did not feel the least bit sick. "I'm all right today," she said. "Always when I've come here before I've felt sick."

He smiled. "You should have put a clean hankie on your stomach," and she was surprised and touched because he did not usually remember much about the past.

"I think it only worked if you got it out of the drawer," she said.

They had reached the stairs and she was about to go up, but he steered her past them, towards another passage.

"Room 17," he said. "The nurse told me."

"Room 17?" Then she realized. "They must have moved her now that she's out of danger. They must really be sure."

He nodded. "The nurse said she'd be very sleepy. She said only to stay a minute."

"She's been on a kind of landing till now." For some reason it seemed important to explain. "Where everyone could see her. And of course she'd throw herself about and groan and I was shouting and trying to get through to her. It was rather horrible."

But they had come to the door of Mama's room and he was not really listening. "All right?" he said with his fingers on the handle, and they went in.

The first thing that struck her was how pretty the room was. It was full of light, with pastel-coloured walls and a big window which overlooked the park. There were flowered curtains, an armchair and a furry rug on the floor. Mama was lying in a neat white bed, untethered, without tubes, one hand tucked under the pillow, the other relaxed on the covers, as Anna had so often seen her in the Putney boarding house, and seemed to be peacefully asleep.

Max was already by the bed.

"Mama," he said.

Mama's eyelids fluttered, sank down again, and finally opened quite normally. For a moment she stared in confusion and then she recognized him.

"Max," she whispered. "Oh, Max." Her blue eyes, the same colour as his, smiled, half-closed, and then opened again full of tears. "I'm so sorry,

Max," she whispered. "Your holiday . . . I didn't mean . . ." Her voice, too, was just as usual.

"That's all right, Mama," said Max. "Everything is all right now."

Her hand moved across the bedclothes into his, and he held it.

"Max," she murmured. "Dear Max . . ." Her eyelids sank down and she went back to sleep.

For a moment, Anna did not know what to do. Then she joined Max at the bed.

"Hello, Mama," she said softly, her lips close to the pillow.

Mama, very sleepy now, hardly reacted. "Anna . . ." Her voice was barely audible. "Are you here too?"

"I've been here since Saturday," said Anna, but Mama was too sleepy to hear her. Her eyes remained closed, and after a while Max disengaged his hand and they went out.

"Is she all right?" he asked. "Is this very different from the way she's been?"

"She's been in a coma for three days," said Anna. "She only came out of it while I was with her last night." She knew it was childish, but she felt put out by the fact that Mama seemed to remember nothing about it. "They told me to keep calling her, so I did, and finally she answered."

"I'm sorry," said Max. "Was it awful?"

"Yes, it was. Like one of those dreadful, corny films."

He laughed a little. "I didn't know they still did that – making you call her. I thought these days it was all done with pills. You may have saved her life."

She was careful not to say so, but secretly she was sure that she had. "It was probably just the German instinct for drama," she said. "I can't imagine them doing it in England, can you? I mean, you wouldn't be allowed into the ward for a start."

They were walking back along the corridor and near the stairs they met the sour-faced nurse of the first day, carrying a bedpan. At the sight of them – or more probably of Max, thought Anna – her mouth relaxed into a smile.

"*Na*," she said in satisfied tones, "*die Frau Mutter ist von den Schatten zurückgekehrt.*"

In English this meant, "So your lady mother has returned from the shadows," and Anna, who had had time to get used to German phraseology, managed to keep a straight face, but, combined with the bedpan, it was too much for Max. He spluttered some kind of agreement and dived round the next corner, Anna following and hoping that the nurse would think he had been overcome with emotion.

"They all talk like that," she giggled when she caught up with him. "Had you forgotten?"

He could only shake his head. "*Aus den Schatten zurückgekehrt* . . . How does Mama stand it?"

She looked at him and began to laugh as well. "*Die Frau Mutter . . .*" she gasped, and even though she knew it was not as funny as all that, it was difficult to stop. She leaned against the wall, clutching his arm for support, and when the nurse came back, without the bedpan this time, they were still laughing so much that they had to pretend to search for something in Anna's bag until she had passed, only to explode again immediately afterwards.

"Oh, Max," cried Anna at last without knowing exactly what she meant, "oh, Max, you're the only one."

It was something to do with their childhood, with having grown up speaking three different languages, with having had to worry so much about Mama and Papa and to cheer themselves up with trilingual jokes which nobody else could understand.

"There, there, little man," said Max, patting her arm. "So are you."

They were still laughing a little when they emerged into the entrance hall, even more crowded now. Konrad and the doctor were already talking together in a corner, and the nurse behind the desk smiled and pointed them out to Max, in case he had not seen them. But Konrad who must have been watching for them, came to meet them and clasped Max warmly by the hand.

"It's good to see you, Max," he said. "I'm sorry we had to drag you away from Greece, but right until this morning it's been touch and go with your mother."

"Of course," said Max. "Thank you for coping with it all."

"*Nu*," said Konrad in tones reminiscent of the Goldblatts, "at my age you learn to cope with everything."

There was an awkwardness between them, and he turned to Anna with evident relief. "That's quite a change of expression you've got there."

"I told you Mama would be all right," she said happily, and by this time they had reached the doctor, and Konrad introduced him to Max, and Max thanked him for all he had done for Mama.

"I believe you've had a long journey," said the doctor, and Max told him a little about it, but quickly brought the conversation back to Mama.

"We were lucky," said the doctor. "I told your sister –" he spread his fingers as he had done the previous day. "Fifty-fifty, didn't I tell you?"

Anna nodded. It seemed a long time ago.

"Yes," said the doctor. "Fifty-fifty. Of course in such a case one does not always know what the patient's wishes would have been. But one has to assume . . . to hope . . ." He discovered his fingers, still in mid-air, and lowered them to his sides.

Behind him, Anna could see a very old lady walking carefully with a stick, and a small boy with his arm in a sling. She was aware of a woolly smell from Konrad's coat, the warmth of a nearby radiator and the babble of German voices all around her, and she felt suddenly tired and remote. Mama is going to be all right, she thought, nothing else matters. For some reason, she remembered again how Mama had looked that time when she had cried in her blue hat with the veil. The veil had been quite wet and had got more and more wrinkled as Mama rubbed her eyes with her hand. When on earth was that? she wondered.

Konrad coughed and shifted his feet. ". . . can't thank you enough . . ." said Max in his very good German, and Konrad nodded and said, ". . . deeply grateful . . ." "After a few days in the clinic to recover . . ." The doctor waved his hands and there seemed to be a question hanging in the air. Then Konrad said loudly and firmly, "Of course I shall be responsible for her." She glanced at him quickly to see if he meant it. His face looked quite set.

The doctor was clearly relieved. So was Max who, she noticed, now looked rather pale and suddenly said, "I've eaten nothing since yesterday lunch time. D'you think I could possibly get breakfast anywhere?"

At this the group broke up.

They all thanked the doctor again, and then she and Max were following Konrad down the steps to his car and Konrad was saying, "You must remember to shake hands with the Germans, otherwise they think you despise them for having lost the War," which seemed so eccentric that she thought she must have misheard until she caught Max's eye and quickly looked away for fear of getting the giggles again.

She stared out of the window while Konrad drove and made various arrangements with Max

– it was cold, but quite a nice day, she discovered – and did not really come to until she found herself sitting at a café table, with the smell of sausages and coffee all round her and Max saying, evidently for the second or third time, "Are you sure you don't want anything to eat?"

He himself was polishing off a large plateful of frankfurters and fried potatoes, and there was a cup of coffee in front of her, so she drank some of that and smiled and shook her head.

"Konrad is going to ring the theatre from his office," said Max, "so that they'll be expecting us."

"The theatre?"

"Where they've got the exhibition about Papa."

"Of course." She had forgotten all about it.

"It's really over. Konrad thought they might even have begun to dismantle it. But the stuff should still be there, and Konrad is going to ring the caretaker to make sure he lets us in."

He looked his normal self again, and she asked, "Are you feeling better now?"

He nodded, his mouth full of frankfurters. "Just reaction," he said. "No food and not enough sleep."

She felt very glad that they were going to see the exhibition together. Suddenly it seemed exactly the right thing to do. "It'll be good to see something to do with Papa," she said.

They had to travel on the *U-Bahn* to get there, but Konrad had explained the route to Max, and he had also given him a map. If you stayed on the train too long, it took you right out of the Western Sector into the Russian Zone and Anna, who considered this a very real danger, watched the stations anxiously and was standing by the doors, ready to get off, when they reached the one they wanted.

"They warn you before you ever get near the Russian Zone," said Max as they climbed up the stairs to the street. "They have big notices at the previous station and announcers and loud-speakers. You couldn't possibly go across by mistake."

She nodded, but did not really believe him. Once, a few months after escaping from Germany, they had changed trains in Basle on their way to Paris with Papa, and they had discovered only at the very last minute that it was the wrong train.

"Do you remember in Basle," she said, "when we nearly got on a train that was going to Germany? We didn't even have time to get the luggage off, and you shouted until someone threw it out to us."

"Did I?" said Max, pleased with his past activity, but, as usual, he had forgotten it.

The theatre was in a busy, unfamiliar street, but then all the streets except the few round her old home and school were unfamiliar to her, thought Anna. There was some heavy bomb damage nearby, but the building itself had either escaped or had been carefully repaired.

They went up some stone steps to the entrance,

knocked and waited. For a long time nothing happened. Then, through a glass panel in the door, they could see an old man coming slowly towards them across the gloom of the foyer. A key ground in the lock, the door opened, and he became clearly visible in the light from the street – very old, very bent, and with a long, grey face that did not look as though it ever went out.

"*Kommen Sie rein, kommen Sie rein*," he said impatiently, rather like the witch, thought Anna, beckoning Hansel and Gretel into the gingerbread house, and he led them slowly across the thick red carpet of the foyer towards a curving staircase.

As he tottered ahead of them, he talked unceasingly. "Can't put the lights on," he said in his heavy Berlin accent. "Not in the morning. Regulations don't allow it." He stopped suddenly and pointed to a chandelier above their heads. "Well, look at it. Set you back a bit to have that shining away, wouldn't it? Real gold, that is."

He tottered off again, muttering about the regulations which seemed to present a major problem, but resolved it to his satisfaction as, with infinite slowness, he climbed the stairs one step at a time. "Put the lights on *upstairs*," he said. "Nothing in the regulations against that."

On a small landing halfway up, he stopped again to get his breath. Anna caught Max's eye, but there was nothing to be done and they had to wait alongside him.

"Used to check the tickets," said the old man. "In the old days. Before it was all took over by

113

them in brown." He flashed a look at Max. "You know who I mean, don't you?"

Max said, yes, he knew whom he meant.

The old man nodded, satisfied. "Used to stand down there at the entrance of the stalls, and see them all go in," he said. "All the gentlemen in their dinner suits and the ladies in their dresses. Quite grand, they was."

He sighed and started again on his slow climb, muttering to himself. A poster with Papa's name and "Exhibition" appeared in the half-darkness. "The great writer and critic", it said underneath.

"Used to see *him*," said the old man, jabbing a finger in its direction. "Come quite often, he did."

They looked at each other. "Did you?" said Anna.

He seemed to think that she was doubting him. "Well, of course I did," he said. "Used to check his ticket. Middle of the third row, he used to sit, never nowhere else, so he could write his little piece in the paper next day. And the others, they used to be real frightened of what he'd put. Once I fetch him a taxi to go home in after the show, and the manager, he come out of the theatre just as he drives off and he says to me, 'Herr Klaube,' he says, 'that man can make or break the play.' A real nice gentleman, I always thought, always thanked me and give me a tip."

Anna saw Max's face in the half-darkness. They both wanted the old man to go on talking about Papa at that time which they were too young to remember. She searched her mind for something to ask him.

"What –" she said, "what did he look like?"

He clearly thought it a stupid question. "Well," he said, "he look like they all look in them days, didn't he. He had one of them cloaks and a stick and a silk hat." Perhaps he sensed her disappointment, for he added, "Anyway, there's plenty of pictures of him in there."

They had arrived at a door with another, bigger, poster on it, and he unlocked it and switched on the lights, while Max pressed a coin into his hand.

"Thank you, sir. I'll drink to you with that," he said as, perhaps, he had said to Papa thirty-odd years before, and tottered back into the semi-darkness of the stairs.

The room he had opened for them was the circle bar, and now that the lights were on, she saw that the walls, not only in the bar but also in the passage outside it, were hung with photographs and reproductions. There was Papa with Einstein, Papa with Bernard Shaw, Papa making a speech, Papa and Mama in America with skyscrapers behind them, Papa and Mama on the deck of an ocean liner. Mama looked like herself, only younger and happier, but Papa seemed unfamiliar because of his habit, which Anna now remembered, of putting on a special expression for photographers.

There were framed newspaper cuttings with explanations beneath them. "The article which caused such controversy in 1927", "The last article to be published before he left Germany in 1933". There were drawings and cartoons, a magazine Papa had edited ("I didn't know he'd done that," said Anna), framed pages of manuscript with his familiar, spidery writing, endlessly corrected.

She looked at it all, touched and bewildered. "It's so strange, isn't it," she said. "All the time he was doing this, we hardly knew him."

"I remember people asking about him at school," said Max.

"And visitors coming to the house. There was a man who brought us some marzipan pigs. I remember Mama saying that he was very famous. I suppose it might have been Einstein."

"I think I would have remembered Einstein," said Max who had forgotten even the marzipan pigs.

Already half dismantled against the wall was a glass case with a complete set of Papa's books. They looked clean and almost unused – very different from his own shabby collection in the Putney boarding house. He had had to acquire the volumes piecemeal from friends who had managed somehow to smuggle them out of Germany.

"He never did get a full set together for himself, did he?" said Max.

"No." She touched the glass case gently with her hand. "No, he never did."

From the far end of the bar, steps led to another passage, and here, too, exhibits had already been taken down and were leaning in a corner, face to the wall. She picked one up at random. It was an enlarged reproduction of a recent article assessing Papa's work. She read, ". . . one of the most brilliant minds of his generation. The books, classics of their kind, are in every university library." In another case nearby were the two thick modern volumes with his collected writings which Mama had worked so hard to get republished the previous year.

"Look at this," said Max. He had found a photograph of the four of them in the garden in Berlin, Papa posing like an author as usual, Mama smiling radiantly, and herself and Max in matching striped woollies, Max with a Christopher Robin haircut on a scooter, herself on a tricycle.

"I remember that being taken," she said. "I remember I'd just got the tricycle, and I was trying to look like someone who could ride a tricycle round corners."

Max considered it. "It doesn't really come across," he said, and added, "actually, you look exactly like Papa."

Suddenly there were no more exhibits, and it seemed they had come to the end of the show.

"That's it," said Max. "It's not really very big, is it?"

They went to the end of the passage, through a door, and found themselves at the back of the circle, a curve of empty red seats sloping down on each side of them. In the vast dimness under the roof hung the usual theatre smell of glue and plaster, and from the well of the stalls came the hum of a vacuum cleaner. Peering down, Anna could see a foreshortened figure Hoovering along the aisle. She looked at the middle of the third row and tried to imagine Papa sitting there, but she couldn't bring him to life.

"It's really just something for people to look at in the interval," said Max, beside her. "But I think it must have been quite effective before they took half of it down."

She nodded and turned to go back the way they had come – and there, between two exits, like a saint in a niche, almost life-size and smiling, was Papa. He was wearing his old grey hat and the shabby winter coat which he had had as long as Anna could remember, and he seemed to be in the middle of saying something. His eyes were focused with interest on something or someone just to one side of the camera, and he looked stimulated and full of life.

She knew the picture, of course, though she had never seen it so enlarged. It had been taken by a press photographer as Papa stepped off the plane in Hamburg on that day long ago – the last picture taken of him before his death. Papa had not known that the photographer was there, so he had not had time to put on his special expression and looked exactly as Anna remembered him.

"Papa," she said.

Max, following her glance, stopped halfway up the steps, and they stood looking at it together.

"It's a perfect place to put it," she said at last. "Looking out over the theatre."

There was a pause. The whine of the Hoover continued to rise from the stalls.

"You know," said Max, "this is the one thing here that really means anything to me. Of course the rest is very interesting, but this, to me, is Papa. What I find so strange is that to everyone else he was someone quite different."

She nodded. "I haven't even read everything he wrote."

"Nor have I."

"The point about Papa –" For a moment she lost track of what the point was. Something to do with having loved Papa when he was old and unsuccessful and yet more interesting than anyone else she knew. "He never felt sorry for himself," she said, but it was not what she meant.

"The point about Papa," said Max, "was not just his work but the sort of person he was."

When they started back down the curved staircase, there were signs of activity in the foyer. The doors to the street were open, someone had taken over the glass-fronted ticket office, and an elderly man was trying to make a booking. They had reached the foot of the stairs, when a gaunt young woman appeared from nowhere, said something about *Kulturbeziehungen* and shook them warmly by the hand.

"Did you enjoy it?" she cried. "I'm so sorry I

wasn't here to meet you. I do hope the janitor – he remembers your father, you know. Your mother came when it opened, of course, and seemed quite pleased, but one always wonders. There is so little room, so one had to select."

"I thought it was excellent," said Max, and she lit up, as people always did when he smiled at them, and straightaway looked less gaunt.

"Did you?" she said. "Did you really? One hopes so much always to have got it right."

"I wish he could have seen it himself," said Anna.

Later, over lunch in a small bar, they talked about Mama.

"It rather hits one," said Max, "when one's seen this exhibition – the sort of person Papa was and the sort of life she used to lead with him. And now she tries to kill herself over someone like Konrad."

"He made her feel safe," said Anna.

"Oh I know, I know."

"I like Konrad," said Anna. "What I find so amazing is the way Mama talks about the things they do together. You know – 'we won three dollars at bridge and the car did eighty miles in an hour and a half' – it's all so boring and ordinary."

Max sighed. "I suppose that's why she likes it. She's never had a chance to do it before."

"I suppose so."

Max sighed again. "Papa was a great man. He took quite a bit of living up to. Being married to him *and* being a refugee – it would make anyone long for some ordinariness. I think in a way we all did."

Anna remembered a time at her English boarding school when she had wished for nothing so much as to be called Pam and to be good at lacrosse. It had been a short-lived phase.

"Not you so much, perhaps," said Max. "If one wants to paint or write, perhaps being different matters less. But me –"

"Nonsense," said Anna. "You've always been different."

He shook his head. "Only in quality. Best student, scholarship winner, brilliant young barrister tipped to be youngest Q.C. –"

"Are you?"

He grinned. "Maybe. But it's all conforming, isn't it? What I'm really doing is making damned sure that in the end I shall be indistinguishable from the very best ordinary people in the country. I've sometimes wondered, if we hadn't been refugees –"

"You'd always have done law. You've got a huge talent for it."

"Probably. But I might have done it for slightly different reasons." He made a face. "No, I can understand exactly why Mama wants to be ordinary."

They sat in silence for a while. At last Anna said, "What do you think will happen now?"

He shrugged his shoulders. "Konrad keeps saying he'll assume complete responsibility for her. I don't know whether that means he wants to pick up where they left off, as though nothing at all had happened. I suppose he may say something when we have dinner tonight."

"Yes." She suddenly saw Mama very clearly, with her vulnerable blue eyes, the determined mouth, the childish snub nose. "She'll be desperate if he doesn't."

"Well, I think he might. I think he means to. What I'm frightened of is that he might feel we're just taking him for granted, and that he'll be put off. I think he'll want some support."

"We could give him that, surely?"

He said nothing for a moment. Then he looked at her. "I left Wendy and the baby on a remote Greek island. I can't stay long."

"I see." It hadn't occurred to her, and she felt suddenly depressed. "Perhaps –" she said, "I suppose I could stay on a few days on my own –" But she hated even the thought of it.

"If you could, it would make all the difference."

"I'd have just to think about it. I've got this new job, you see. It's quite important." The new job and Mama were jumbled up in confusion. Back to Mama, thought part of her mind with the usual sense of panic, and another part thought of Richard, but he seemed far away. "I'd want first to talk to Richard about it."

"Well, of course," he said.

He looked white again when the waitress brought the bill, and said, "Do you mind if we go back to the hotel? I've had practically no sleep for two nights and I suddenly feel rather tired. Konrad said he'd fixed up a room for me."

While he slept, she lay on her bed and stared at the patterned curtains as they moved very gently in the draught. She wished that she had not mentioned staying on. Now it would be difficult not to do it, she thought, feeling mean. And yet, she thought, why should it always be me? Still, she hadn't actually committed herself, and at the worst it would only be a few days. I simply wouldn't stay longer than that, she told herself. For a moment she considered trying to ring Richard. But it would be best to talk to Konrad first. After all, now that Mama was out of danger, he might not even want anyone to stay.

The patterned curtains moved and flowed. She felt suddenly sharply aware of herself, of the shabby German house around her and of Max resting in the next room. There was Konrad in his office and his secretary watching him, and Mama waking up properly at last from her long anaesthesia and Richard trying to write his script and waiting for her in London, and in the past, behind them all, was Papa.

This, she thought, is what it's like. She felt that she could see it all, every bit of it in relation to the rest, and she knew everybody's thoughts and all their feelings, and could set them off against each other with hair-trigger precision. I could write about it all, she thought. But the thought was so cold-blooded that she shocked herself and tried to pretend that she had not had it.

* * *

They went to the hospital in the late afternoon, and when they opened the door of Mama's room, they found Konrad already there. He was sitting on the bed, and Mama, who looked tense and on the edge of tears, was holding his hand. Her blue eyes were fixed on his and she had put on some lipstick, which looked strangely bright in her exhausted face.

"*Nu*," said Konrad, "here are your children who have come from all the corners of the earth to see you, so I'll leave you."

"Don't go." Mama's voice was still a little faint. "Must you?"

"Yes, ma'am, I must," said Konrad. He heaved his bulk off the bed and smiled his asymmetrical smile. "I shall go for a walk, which is good for me, which is why I so rarely do it, and then I shall come back and buy your children some dinner. In the meantime, you behave yourself."

"Don't walk too far."

"No, ma'am," he said, and Anna saw Mama's mouth quiver as he went out of the room.

"He always calls me ma'am," she said tremulously, as though it explained everything.

They had brought some flowers, and Anna inserted them into a vase which already contained some rather more splendid ones from Konrad, while Max took Konrad's place on the bed.

"Well, Mama," he said with his warm smile. "I'm very glad you're better."

"Yes," said Anna from behind the vase. They

were both afraid that Mama would begin to cry.

She still seemed rather dazed. "Are you?" she said, and then added with more of her normal vigour, "I'm not. I wish they'd just left me alone. It would have been much simpler for everyone."

"Nonsense, Mama," said Max, and at this her eyes filled with tears.

"The only thing I'm sorry about," she said, "is that I dragged you away from your holiday. I didn't want to – I really didn't. But it was so awful –" She sniffed through her little snub nose and searched for a handkerchief under her pillow. "I tried not to," she cried. "I tried to wait at least until you'd be back in London, but each day – I just couldn't bear it any longer." She had found the handkerchief and blew into it, hard. "If only they'd just let me die," she said, "then you needn't have come until the funeral, and perhaps you could have finished your holiday first."

"Yes, Mama," said Max. "But I might not have enjoyed it very much."

"Wouldn't you?" She saw his face, and her voice warmed to something almost like a giggle. "After all, what's an old mother?"

"True, Mama. But I just happen to be attached to mine, and so is Anna."

"Yes," said Anna, through the flowers.

"Oh, I don't know, I don't know."

She lay back on the pillow and closed her eyes, and tears damped her cheeks from under the closed lids.

"I'm so tired," she said.

Max patted her hand. "You'll feel better soon."

But she seemed not to hear him. "Did he tell you what he'd done?" she said. "He got another girl."

"But it didn't mean anything," said Anna. She had squatted down near the bed, and at the sight of Mama's tear-stained face on a level with her own, as she had so often seen it from her bed in the Putney boarding house, the familiar feeling rose up inside her that she could not bear Mama to be so unhappy, that it must somehow be stopped.

Mama looked at her. "She was younger than me."

"Yes, but Mama –"

"You don't know what it's like," cried Mama. "You're young yourself, you've got your Richard." She turned her face away and cried, to the wall, "Why couldn't they have let me die? They let Papa die in peace – I arranged that. Why couldn't they have let me?"

Anna and Max exchanged glances.

"Mama –" said Max.

Anna discovered that she had pins and needles and stood up. She did not like to rub her leg, in case it looked callous, so she went over to the window and stood there miserably, flexing and unflexing her knee.

"Look, Mama, I know you've had a bad time, but I think everything is going to be all right. After all, you and Konrad have been together a long time." Max was talking in his reasonable lawyer's voice.

"Seven years," said Mama.

"There you are. And this affair, whatever it was, meant nothing to him. He's said so. And when people have had as good and as long a relationship as you two, you can survive a lot more troubles than that."

"We did have a good relationship," said Mama. "We made a good team. Everybody said so."

"There you are, then."

"Did you know that we were runners-up in the bridge tournament? With lots of American and English couples competing, all very practised players. And we should really have tied with the couple who won, only there was a stupid rule –"

"You've always been terribly good together."

"Yes," said Mama. "For seven years." She looked at Max. "How could he smash it all up? How could he?"

"I think it was something that just happened."

But she was not listening. "The holidays we had together," she said. "When we first got the car and went to Italy. He drove and I map read. And we found this lovely little place by the sea – I sent you photographs, didn't I? We were so happy. And it wasn't just me, it was him, at least as much. He told me so. He said, 'Never in all my life have I been as happy as I am now.' His wife was very dull, you see. They never did anything or went anywhere. All she ever wanted to do was to buy more furniture."

Max nodded, and Mama's blue eyes, fixed on some distant memory, suddenly returned to him.

"This girl," she said, "The one he had an affair with. Did you know she was German?"

"No," said Max.

"Well, she is. A little German secretary. Very little education, speaks very bad English, and she's not even pretty. Only –" Mama's eyes became wet again – "only younger."

"Oh, Mama, I'm sure that's nothing to do with it."

"Well, what else is it to do with, then? It must have been something. You don't smash up seven years of happiness just for no reason!"

Max took her hand. "Look, Mama, there was no reason. It was just something that happened. It was never important to him, except for the way you reacted. Anyway, he's been here. Didn't he tell you so himself?"

"Yes," said Mama in a small voice. "But how do I know it's true?"

"I think it's true," said Anna. "I've been with him for two days, and I think it's true."

Mama glanced at her briefly and then looked back at Max.

"I think so too," said Max. "And I'll be seeing him tonight. I'll talk to him and find out what he really thinks, and I promise I'll tell you exactly what he said. But I'm sure it'll be all right."

Mama, her eyes finally brimming over, sank back into the pillows.

"Oh, Max," she said. "I'm so glad you're here."

★ ★ ★

Later, in the car, Anna stared out at the rubble and the half-made new buildings flying past in the light of the street lamps and wondered how it was all going to end. Konrad was driving, carefully and efficiently as usual, and she suddenly felt she had no idea what he was thinking. He seemed to be taking them on a tour of the city and, with Max on the front seat beside him, was pointing out various landmarks.

"*Kurfürsten Damm . . . Leibnitz Strasse . . . Gedächtnis Kirche . . . Potsdamer Platz . . .*"

She could see soldiers, some kind of a barrier and above it, carefully lit, a sign saying, "You are now leaving the American Sector". It looked cold and dark. Some young people, gathered in a group, were flapping their arms and stamping their feet. Most of them were carrying placards and, as she watched, they suddenly moved closer to the barrier and all shouted together, "*Russen raus! Russen raus! Russen raus!*"

Konrad caught her eyes in the driving mirror. "Supporters for Hungary," he said. "I can't see it having much effect, but it's nice to see them try."

She nodded. "There are a lot of them in London, too."

The *Potsdamer Platz* faded behind them.

"Do the Russians ever retaliate?" asked Max.

"Not by shouting slogans. There are more effective ways, such as doubling the checks on the road in and out of Berlin. That means everything takes twice as long to get through."

The shouts of *"Russen raus!"* could still be faintly heard in the distance. A group of American soldiers marching in step, steel-helmeted and armed, flickered momentarily into vision, to disappear again into the darkness.

"Doesn't it ever bother you, being surrounded like this? I mean," said Anna, "suppose the Russians attacked?" She tried to sound detached, without success.

Max grinned at her over his shoulder. "Don't worry, little man. I promise they won't get you."

"If the Russians attacked," said Konrad, "they could take Berlin in ten minutes. Everyone who lives here knows this. The reason they don't attack is because they know that if they did, they would find themselves at war with the Americans."

"I see."

"And even to get you, little man," said Max, "they won't risk starting a third world war."

She laughed half-heartedly. It was cold in the back of the car and as Konrad turned a corner, she suddenly felt queasy. Not again! she thought.

Konrad was watching her in the driving mirror.

"Supper," he said. "About three streets from here. I've booked at a restaurant you've been to before – I hope you don't mind, but you enjoyed it last time."

It turned out to be the place where they had celebrated her and Richard's decision to get married, and as soon as she recognized it – the warm, smoky atmosphere, the tables covered with red cloths and separated from each other by high-backed wooden benches – she felt better.

"*Etwas zu trinken?*" asked the fat proprietress. (Last time, Mama having proudly told her what was being celebrated, she had given them schnapps on the house.)

Konrad ordered whisky, and when she brought it she smiled and said in German, "A family reunion?"

"You could call it that," said Konrad and, ridiculous though it was, that was exactly what it felt like.

Konrad sat between them and, like a fond and generous uncle, helped them choose their food from the menu, consulted Max about the wine, worried about their comfort and refilled their glasses. Meanwhile he talked about impersonal subjects – the dubious Russian promise to leave Hungary if the Hungarians laid down their arms, the trouble in Suez, where the Israelis had finally attacked Egypt. ("I hope Wendy won't be too worried," said Max. "After all, Greece isn't very far away.") Then, when they had finished the main course, Konrad sat back as far as it was possible for such a large man to sit back on a narrow wooden bench, and turned to Max.

"Your sister will have given you some idea of what has been happening," he said. "But I expect you'd like to know exactly."

"Yes," said Max. "I would."

"Of course." He placed his knife and fork neatly side by side on his plate. "I don't know if your mother happened to mention it in her letters, but she recently went to Hanover for a few days. It was a special assignment and rather a compliment to her. While she was away I – became involved with someone else."

They both looked at him. There seemed nothing suitable to say.

"This – temporary involvement was not serious. It is now over and done with. I told your mother about it, so that she should not hear about it from anyone else. I thought she would be mature enough to see it in its proper perspective . . ."

(Hold on, thought Anna. Up to now she had been with him, but if he really believed that . . . How could he possibly believe that Mama would take it calmly?)

". . . After all, we're neither of us children."

She looked at him. His kind, middle-aged face had a curious closed expression. Like a small boy, she thought, insisting that taking the watch to pieces could not possibly have damaged it.

"But, Konrad –"

He lost some of his detachment. "Well, she *should* have understood. It was nothing. I told her it was nothing. Look, your mother is an intelligent, vital woman. She has an enormous enjoyment of life, and that's something she's taught me, too, during the past years. All the things we've done together – the friendships, the holidays, even some of the jobs I've held – I would never have done without her. Whereas this other girl – she's a little secretary. She's never been anywhere, never done anything, lives at home with her mother, does the cooking and the mending, hardly speaks . . ."

"Then – why?" asked Max.

"I don't know." He frowned, puzzling it out. "I suppose," he said at last, "I suppose it made a little rest."

It sounded so funny that she found herself laughing. She caught Max's eye, and he was laughing too. It was not just the way Konrad had said it, but that they both knew what he meant.

There was an intensity about Mama which was exhausting. You could never for a moment forget her presence, even when she was content. "Isn't it *lovely!*" she would say, daring you to disagree. "Don't you think this is the most *beautiful* day?" Or place, or meal, or whatever else it was that had made her happy. She would pursue what she believed to be perfection with ruthless energy, battling for the best place on the beach, the right job, an extra day's leave, with a determination which most people could not be bothered to resist.

"It's not your mother's fault," said Konrad. "It's the way she is." He smiled a little. "*Immer mit dem Kopf durch die Wand.*"

"That's what Papa used to say about her," said Anna.

She had tried to translate the expression for Richard. It meant not just banging your head against brick walls, but actually bursting through them head first, as a matter of habit.

"Did he really?" said Konrad. "She never told

me that. But of course she used to do it to very good purpose. Getting you both educated when there was no money. Getting a job without qualifications. I don't suppose that without her habit of bursting through brick walls, either of you would have come through the emigration as well as you did."

"Well, of course." They both knew it and felt it did not need pointing out.

There was a little pause. "But this other girl – the secretary," said Max at last. "What does she feel about it all? Does *she* think it's over?"

Konrad had his closed, little-boy expression again. "I've told her," he said. "I've made quite sure she understands."

Suddenly, out of the smoke and the muddle of German voices, the proprietress bore down on them with coffee and three small glasses.

"A little schnapps," she said, "for the family reunion."

They thanked her, and Konrad made a joke about the burdens of a family man. She burst into laughter and drifted back into the smoke. He turned again to Max.

"And now?" said Max. "What will happen now?"

"Now?" The little-boy look had disappeared and Konrad looked suddenly what he was – a rather plain, elderly Jew who had seen a lot of trouble. "Now we pick up the pieces and put them together again." He raised the little glass and put it to his lips. "To the family reunion," he said.

* * *

Afterwards Anna remembered the rest of the evening like a kind of party. She felt happily confused as though she were drunk, not so much with schnapps as with the knowledge that everything was going to be all right. Mama would get over her unhappiness. Konrad would see to it, as he had always seen to everything. And between them they had all – and especially Anna – saved Mama from dying stupidly, unnecessarily, and in a state of despair for which it would be difficult to forgive oneself.

Max and Konrad, too, seemed in a much more relaxed state. They swapped legal anecdotes without any of the awkwardness that normally came between them, and once, when Anna returned from the Ladies (a very functional place almost entirely filled by one large woman adjusting a hard felt hat over her iron grey hair) she found them roaring with laughter together like old friends.

The mood only began to fade while Konrad drove them home. Perhaps it was the cold, and the sight of the half-built streets with their patrolling soldiers. Or, more likely, thought Anna, it was the realization that it was nearly midnight and too late for her to ring Richard. Whatever it was, she found herself unexpectedly homesick and depressed, and she was horrified when, at the door of the hotel, Konrad suddenly said, "I'm so glad you'll be able to stay on for a while in Berlin. It will make all the difference."

She was too taken aback to say anything in

reply, and it was only after he had gone that she turned angrily to Max. "Did you tell Konrad that I was going to stay on?" she asked.

They were in the little breakfast room which also served as reception area, and a sleepy adolescent girl, no doubt a relation of the owner, was preparing to hand them their keys.

"I don't know – I may have done," said Max. "Anyway, I thought you said you were going to."

"I only said I might." She felt suddenly panicked. "I never said definitely. I said I wanted first to talk to Richard."

"Well, there's nothing to stop you explaining that to Konrad. I don't see why you should be in such a state about it." Max, too, was clearly suffering from reaction, and they stood glaring at each other by the desk.

"Rooms 5 and 6," said the girl, pushing the keys and a piece of paper across to them. "And a telephone message for the lady."

It was from Richard, of course. He had rung up and missed her. The paper contained only his name, grotesquely misspelt. He had not even been able to leave a message, because no one in the hotel spoke English.

"Oh damn, oh damn, oh damn!" she shouted.

"For God's sake," said Max. "He's bound to ring again tomorrow night."

"Tomorrow night I'm going to a bloody party," she shouted. "Konrad arranged that. Everybody here seems to decide exactly what I should be doing at any given time. Perhaps just once in a while I might be consulted. Perhaps next time you make long-term arrangements for me, you might just ask me first."

Max looked confounded. "What party?" he said.

"Oh, what does it matter what party? Some awful British Council thing."

"Look." He spoke very calmly. "You've got this whole thing out of proportion. If you like, I'll explain it to Konrad myself. There simply isn't any problem."

But of course it was not true. It would be much more difficult to tell Konrad that she was not staying, now he believed that she was.

Alone in bed, she thought of London and of Richard, and found to her horror that she could not clearly visualize his face. Her insides contracted. The familiar nausea swept over her, and for a long time she lay under the great quilt in the darkness and listened to the trains rumble along distant tracks. At last she could stand it no longer: she got up, dug in her suitcase for a clean handkerchief, climbed back into bed and spread it on her stomach.

Wednesday

Max could not have slept well either, and they were both bad-tempered at breakfast. They had to wait for their coffee, for the little breakfast room was filled with six or seven guests who must have arrived on the previous day, and even with the help of the adolescent girl, the proprietress was too disorganized to serve them properly.

"When do you expect to leave then?" Anna asked Max coldly.

He made an impatient gesture. "I don't know. But I've got to get back to Greece soon. For God's sake," he said, "nobody there speaks a word of English, Wendy doesn't speak a word of Greek, and she's got a ten-month-old baby."

She said nothing for a moment. Then resentment rose up irresistibly inside her and she said, "It's just that I don't see why it should always be me who has to cope."

"It isn't always you." He was trying to attract the proprietress's attention, without success. "You know perfectly well that even during the war when I was flying, and later when I was working my guts out in Cambridge, I always came home. I came whenever there was a crisis, and I came whenever I could, apart from that, just to lend moral support."

"You came," she said. "But you didn't stay."

"Well, of course I didn't stay. I was supposed to be flying a bloody aeroplane. I was supposed to be getting a First in law and make a career and be a prop to the family."

"Oh, I know, I know." She felt suddenly tired of the argument. "It's just – you can't imagine what it was like being there all the time. The hopelessness of doing anything for Papa, and Mama's depressions. Even then, you know, she was always talking about suicide."

"But she didn't actually do anything, did she?" said Max. "I mean, this *is* a bit different."

She had a sudden vision of Mama in her blue hat, her face wet with tears, saying, "I couldn't go on. I just couldn't go on." In a street somewhere – Putney, she supposed. Why did she keep remembering it? And was it something that had really happened or something she had imagined?

"Anyway," said Max, "if you really want to go back to London, you'll just have to go. Though I wouldn't have thought a few days would have mattered either way."

"Oh, let's wait and see," she said wearily. "Let's see how Mama is this morning."

Max had finally managed to catch the proprietress's eye, and she hurried resentfully over to their table.

"All right, all right," she said. "You're not at war here, you know."

While he ordered the coffee and rolls, Anna made a mental note of the expression – a bit of Berlin dialect which even Heimpi had never used. A German at the next table tittered at the sound of it. Then he smiled at Anna and pointed to his newspaper. "Rule Britannia, eh?" he said. She looked at the front page and read the headline: *Englischer Angriff in Suez*.

"For God's sake, Max," she said. "Look at that. We're at war."

"What?"

"*Bitte, bitte*," said the German and handed the paper over to them.

It was true. British paratroopers were supporting the Israelis in Egypt. There was not much beyond the headline – clearly few details were known as yet – but a longer article speculated on the effect this new development might have on the Hungarian situation. A headline almost as big as the one about Suez said, "Russians offer to withdraw troops from Hungary, Romania and Poland".

"What does it mean?" said Anna, trying to control the panic rising inside her.

Max had his alert lawyer's look, as though in

the few moments since reading about it he had already weighed up the situation.

"One thing is certain," he said. "I've got to get Wendy home."

"What about me? What about here in Berlin?"

"I don't think it'll make any difference here. At least not at the moment. But you'd better ring Richard tonight. He may have a better idea of what's going on."

"The Russians –?"

Max pointed to the paper. "They seem quite conciliatory at the moment. I think they've got their hands full. Look, you hang on for the coffee, I'll just try and ring BEA. God knows how long it'll take to get me to Athens."

She sat at the grubby little table by herself and nervously drank some of the coffee when it came.

"*Bitte?*" said the German, pointing to the paper, and she gave it back to him.

Then Max returned, all energy and bustle. "They said to call in before lunch," he said. "There may be a connecting flight tomorrow. If I can get on that, and if I can contact my ship owner, perhaps he'll arrange transport for me at the other end."

"Max," she said, "couldn't I try and ring Richard now?"

He sat down. "No good, I'm afraid," he said. "I just checked. There's a three hour delay on all calls to London."

"I see."

"Look, there's no question of your staying here in case of any danger. At the smallest hint of anything you get on a plane home. Konrad will see to that, anyway. But I honestly think it's probably as safe here at the moment as it's ever been."

She nodded without conviction.

"Anyway, talk to Richard tonight. And talk to Konrad. If we hurry, we may catch him at the hospital."

However, Konrad had left a message that he had an urgent meeting and would visit Mama in his lunch break. They found her looking physically much like herself but in a desperate state of tension. The nurse was just removing her breakfast tray (anyway, she'd eaten it all, Anna noted with relief) and Mama did not even wait for the door to close behind her before she asked, "Well? What did he say?"

"What did who say?" Max knew perfectly well, of course, but was just trying to slow her down.

"Konrad. What did he say to you last night? What did he say about me?" Her blue eyes stared, her hands drummed nervously on the edge of the sheet. The whole room was filled with her tension.

Max managed to sound easy as he answered. "Mama, he said exactly what I expected, and what he'd already told you. The affair is finished. He wants you back. He wants to forget everything that's happened and to start again where you both left off."

"Oh." She relaxed a little. "But then why didn't he come this morning?"

"He told you. He had a meeting. Perhaps something to do with this Suez business."

"Suez? Oh, that." The nurse must have told her, thought Anna. "But that wouldn't have anything to do with Konrad."

Max's irritation was beginning to show. "It may have nothing to do with Konrad, but it's got something to do with me. I have to get back to Greece as soon as possible and bring Wendy and the baby home. Probably tomorrow. So just for today, can we stop worrying about his every thought and gesture, and talk properly?"

"Wendy and the baby? But why do you have to bring them home? Why can't they just catch a plane on their own?"

They're going to have a row, thought Anna.

"For heaven's sake, Mama, they're on a remote island. Wendy doesn't speak a word of Greek. She couldn't possibly manage."

"Couldn't she?" Mama's anger was mixed with a certain triumph. "Well, I could. When you and Anna were small, I got you both out of Germany without any help from anyone. And before that, for two weeks after Papa had already fled, I kept it a secret and I got you to keep it a secret too – you were only twelve and nine at the time. I packed up our house and all our belongings, and then I got you both out, twenty-four hours before the Nazis came for our passports."

"I know, Mama, you were terribly good. But Wendy is different."

"How different? I'd have liked to be different too. I'd have loved to be different, so that everybody would look after me. Instead, I had to look after everybody else."

"Mama –" But it was no good.

"I cooked and cleaned when we lived in Paris. And then, when Papa could no longer earn anything, I got a job and supported us all. I got you into your English public school –"

"Not quite by yourself, Mama. I must have had something to do with it too."

"You know what I mean. And then, when we could no longer pay the fees, I went to see the headmaster –"

"And he gave me a scholarship. I know, Mama. But it wasn't easy for the rest of us either. It wasn't much fun for Papa, and even Anna and I had our problems."

Mama's hands clenched on the sheet. "But you were young," she cried. "It didn't matter. You had all your lives to come. Whereas I . . . All those years I spent in dreary boarding houses worrying about money, I was getting older. It should have been the best time of my life, and instead I spent it scraping pennies together and worrying myself sick over Papa and Anna and you. And now at last when I'd found someone who looked after me, with whom I could do all the things I'd missed, he had to go and – he had to go and have an affair with a stupid, feeble little German typist." Her voice broke and she wept again.

Anna wondered whether to say anything, but decided not to. Nobody would have listened to her anyway.

"It wasn't like that, Mama. It's never as simple as that." Max looked as though he had been wanting to say this for years. "You always over-simplify."

"But I did do those things. I did keep everything going. When we first came to England and still had some money, it was I who decided that we should send you to a public school, and I was right – you'd never have done so well if we hadn't."

"It might have been more difficult."

"And your headmaster told me – I always remember what he said about you. He said, 'He's got a first-class brain, he's hard-working and he's got charm. There's nothing he won't be able to do. He can be Prime Minister if he wants."

"He couldn't really have said that," Max was quivering on the edge of a grin. "I mean, old Chetwyn – it wasn't his style."

"But he did, he did! And he said what a good mother I was. And I remember at Christmas, when I still had that good job with Lady Parker, and she asked me what I'd like for a Christmas present, and I said, 'I'd like a radio for my son,' and she said, 'Wouldn't you like something for yourself, a dress or a coat?' and I said, 'It's the one thing he wants, if I can give him that it'll be better than anything,' and she said –"

"Oh, I know, Mama, I know –"

"And during the war, when you were interned, Papa just wanted to let matters take their course, but I *made* him write to the papers, it was me who got you out, if it hadn't been for me you'd have been there much longer. And it was me who found the secretarial school for Anna, and then, when you were in the Air Force and you had trouble with that girl, I coped with it, I went to see her –"

"I know, Mama, it's all true –"

Mama's face was red and tearful like a very small child's. "I *was* a good mother!" she cried. "I know I was! Everybody said what a good mother I was!"

"Well, of course you were," said Max.

It was suddenly quiet.

"But then, why," said Mama, "why is everything now so awful?"

"I don't know," said Max. "Perhaps because we've grown up."

They looked at each other with their identical blue eyes, and Anna thought how often in Putney, in Bloomsbury, even in Paris, she had sat through scenes like this. The arguments had been different each time, but always there had been, amidst the shouting and the anger, the same sense of closeness between them, something which left no room for anyone else. As now, she had sat silent on the edge, watching Mama's face, noting (even then?) the exact words of her accusations and of Max's replies. In those days, of course, there had been Papa to stop her from feeling entirely left out.

"You see," said Max, "in a way it was all exactly as you say. But it was also quite different."

"How?" cried Mama. "In what way? How could it have been?"

He frowned, searching for the right phrases. "Well, it's quite true, of course, that I've been a success, and that without you, it would have been much more difficult."

"Very much more difficult," said Mama, but he ignored her.

"But at the same time, it wasn't all for me. I mean, in a way, perhaps because everything was so awful for you, you needed me to be a success."

Mama drummed irritably on the sheet. "Well, why shouldn't I? For God's sake, do you remember how we used to live? I'd have done anything – anything – for Papa to have had even a little bit of success in those days."

"No, you don't understand. What I mean is – because you needed it so much, every little thing I did had to be, somehow, a triumph. I used to hear you talking about me. You used to say, 'He's going to stay with friends, they've got an estate in the country.' Well, it wasn't. It was a boy in Esher, I liked him very much, but he lived in a semi-detached. The only time I went anywhere grand while I was at school, my suitcase burst when the butler tried to unpack it, and the father, Sir Something-or-other, had to give me one of his, which he hated. It was all very embarrassing, but the way you told it, it was, 'And this lord took such a fancy to

Max that he insisted on giving him some of his own luggage.'"

Mama looked puzzled and upset. "Well, what does it matter – little things like that? And anyway, he probably did like you. People always do."

Max sighed impatiently. "But it was other things as well. You used to say, 'Of course he'll get a scholarship, of course he'll get a first.' Well, I did get them, but there was no of course about it. I had to work very hard, and I often worried about whether I'd make it."

"Well, perhaps – it's possible." Mama's mouth was pulled down obstinately at the corners. "But I still don't see that it matters."

"It matters because it made it difficult for me to see my life as it really was. And it matters now because you're doing the same thing to yourself. Re-shaping things if they don't fit. Everything black and white. No uncertainties, no failures, no mistakes."

"Nonsense," said Mama, "I don't do that at all." She was getting tired and her voice rose. "You don't know how I live here," she cried. "Everybody likes me, they all like talking to me and even ask me for advice. *They* don't think I see everything in black and white. I've got quite a reputation for solving people's problems, love affairs, all sorts of things." She finally burst into tears. "You don't know anything about me!" she cried.

Sooner or later it always came to this, thought Anna. She was relieved to see a nurse appear at the door with a cup of soup.

"Zur guten Besserung," said the nurse, and they all watched, Mama sniffing and blowing her nose, while she crossed the room and put the soup on the bedside table and went out again.

"Anyway, I was quite right," said Mama almost before she had left. "It's all happened just as I said. You do know all sorts of lords and people like that, and you *are* making a great career."

"Yes, Mama." Max was tired too. He patted her arm. "I must go soon," he said. "I've got to do something about my ticket."

She clutched his hand. "Oh, Max!"

"There, there, Mama. You're a very good mother, and everything will be all right." They smiled at each other, cautiously, with their identical blue eyes.

Anna, smiled too, just to be companionable, and wondered whether she should leave with Max when he went or stay with Mama and wait for Konrad. It would be difficult to know what to say, she thought. After the excitement of Max, anything she might think of would come as an anti-climax. On the other hand, if she stayed, she might be able to talk to Konrad about going home.

Mama was still holding Max's hand. "How was it in Greece?" she said.

"Absolutely marvellous." He began to tell her about the case he was doing, and about the ship owner's seaside house. ". . . right on the beach of this tiny island, with a cook and God knows how many servants. He owns it all – the whole place.

He's got olive groves and his own vineyard, all incredibly beautiful, and we had the run of it. The only trouble was, Wendy was a bit worried about the greasy food for the baby."

"Did you swim?"

"Three times a day. The sea is so warm and so clear —"

But, unexpectedly, Mama's eyes had filled with tears. "Oh, Max, I'm so sorry," she cried. "I didn't mean to interrupt your holiday. I didn't mean to drag you away to Berlin."

Anna suddenly felt childishly angry.

"What about me?" she said, startling all three of them, since she had said nothing for so long. "What about dragging me to Berlin from London?"

"You?" Mama looked surprised and upset. "I thought you might quite like to come."

"Quite like . . . ?" She was almost speechless.

"I mean, you weren't doing anything special, and I knew you hadn't been away in the summer."

There was a trace of a query in Mama's voice, and Anna found herself answering, in spite of herself, "I've got a new job, and Richard is in the middle of writing a serial." It sounded so feeble that she stopped, and fury overcame her. After all I've done, she thought. After sitting on her bed and dragging her out of her coma. But even while she was thinking it, another part of herself was coolly noting Mama's exact words, as it had already noted much of the conversation. If one were really going to write about this, she thought guiltily, they would make a marvellous bit of dialogue.

In the end she left the sickroom with Max and waited for Konrad in the reception hall. Through one of the windows, she watched him park his car in the drive, hesitate whether or not to bring his stick, and finally walk up towards the entrance without it. He manoeuvred his bulk through the swing doors and smiled when he saw her.

"Hullo," he said. "How's your mother?"

"I'm not sure," she said. "We had a row."

"*Nu*," he said, "if she could have a row, she must be feeling better." He looked at her. "Was it serious?"

"Not really, I suppose. It was mostly with Max, and I don't think she minds that so much. I only came in at the end."

"I see. And is that why you waited for me here?"

"No." She decided to take the bull by the horns. "It's this Suez business. Max is worried about Wendy and the baby, and he's gone to try and book a flight to Athens. And I just wondered –"

"What?"

A woman with a bandaged hand said, "*Verzeihung*," and pushed past them, giving her time to choose her words.

"What do you think?" she said. "Might there be trouble here? I mean, I suppose all this is bound to affect the Russians." She added quickly, before he could answer, "Richard rang me last night, but I missed him. I expect he may be worried."

"Yes," he said, considering her. "Yes, I suppose he may be."

"Of course I don't mean that I want to rush off at once or anything. It's just that – it seems impossible to get through to London in the daytime," she said. "D'you think I could ring Richard from the party tonight? Just to know what he thinks?"

"Well, of course," he said. "There'll be no difficulty about that."

"Oh, good."

There was a pause.

"I don't think the Suez business represents any kind of threat in Berlin at the moment," he said at last. "But I can see that for you there may be other considerations."

"It's really Richard," she said. "I wouldn't want him to worry."

He nodded, looking tired. "I'd better go and see your mother. You ring Richard tonight, and then we'll talk."

She felt guilty while she sat on the bus to the *Kurfürsten Damm* where she was to meet Max for lunch. But it's not as though I'd said I was leaving, she told herself, I was only asking his advice.

Even so, the memory of his tired face stayed with her. As she waited for Max, she stood staring into a newly-built shop window filled with garishly checked materials. "Genuine English Tartans" said a sign in German, and they had names like

Windsor, Eton and Dover. One was even called Sheffield. Richard would enjoy that, she thought, but instead of feeling amused she found herself fretting about Konrad. I'll see, she thought. I'll see what happens tonight.

Max arrived, full of energy and confidence as always, and swept her off to a nearby café.

"I've booked a flight," he announced before they had even sat down. "It connects with a flight from Paris to Athens. I also got them to let me use their telephone and got through to my ship owner, and he's arranging for someone to meet me at the airport."

"I'm glad," said Anna.

"Yes." He added as an afterthought, "My ship owner also thought it was urgent to get Wendy and the baby out of there."

She nodded. "When do you go?"

"At one o'clock in the morning."

"What – tonight?"

"That's right. Well," he said, "it really makes no difference. I couldn't have seen Mama tomorrow anyway, unless I'd stayed till the afternoon, and that would have been too late. I thought I'd see her again later today and stay a long time, however long one is allowed, till she goes to sleep. And then – well, I could come to the party and go straight to the airport from there."

"Yes, I suppose so." As so often with Max, she was left far behind, still feeling her way round a situation which he had long assessed. "Have you told Konrad?"

"Not yet, but he'll know from Mama that I'm probably leaving. Did you have a chance to speak to him?"

"Only for a moment." She did not want to go into details. "He said we'd talk tonight."

"Good. And you're going to ring Richard?"

"Yes."

He smiled his confident, warm, affectionate smile. "Well," he said, "I'd better go and pack my things."

Max's last evening with Mama was very harmonious. Mama looked pink and relaxed. She had been reassured by Konrad's visit at lunch time – he had stayed almost two hours and they had obviously talked things out – and afterwards she had slept. When Anna and Max arrived, she had only just woken up and was still nestling deep in the pillows, looking up from beneath the big white quilt like a baby from its cot.

"Hullo," she said, and smiled.

Her smile was as warm as Max's, but without his confidence. No grown-up person, thought Anna, should look so vulnerable.

She was less upset than they had expected by the news of Max's departure, and quite pleased with the dramatic manner of it. "You're going to the party first?" she kept saying admiringly, and when a nurse looked in to collect a dirty towel, she insisted on introducing him and saying, "He's flying to Athens tonight."

"And how was Konrad?" asked Max after the nurse had gone.

"Oh –" Mama's smile softened and she sniffed

a little with emotion. "I really think it's going to be all right. We talked for ages. He explained it all to me again, about this girl. It really didn't mean anything to him. It was just because I was away and he missed me. Frankly, I think it was largely her doing. She sounds," said Mama, "a rather predatory creature."

"I'm so glad it's all right."

"Yes, well, of course we'll have to see." But her eyes were bright. "He wants us to go away on a holiday together," she said. "As soon as I'm better. The doctor thinks I should stay here for a few days, and then maybe a week in a convalescent home." She made a face. "God knows how much it'll all cost. But after that – we thought, not Italy at this time of year, but perhaps somewhere in the Alps."

"It sounds a very good idea."

"Yes." Her lip quivered for a moment. "I think I probably need it. It's all been quite a shock."

"Of course."

"Yes. The doctor says I'm lucky to have come through it. He says I nearly died." She shrugged her shoulders. "I still think it might have been best."

"Nonsense, Mama," said Max.

Mama looked suddenly very pleased.

"It seems," she said, "that anyone less strong than me certainly would have done."

Later the conversation drifted to the past. "Do you remember?" said Mama: How she used to buy

155

bruised strawberries in Paris for almost nothing and cut off the bad bits to make a delicious Sunday pudding. The bomb that wrecked their Bloomsbury boarding house. The last years in Putney.

"You had a blue hat with a veil," said Anna.

"That's right. I got it at C and A, and everyone thought it came from Bond Street."

"That woman who ran the boarding house – she used to put a camp bed up for me when I came to visit and never charged me," said Max. "She was a very decent soul."

"She ended up by marrying one of the guests, a Pole. Do you remember, the one who made the bird noises? We used to call him the Woodpigeon."

"It was all quite funny, really," said Anna, but Mama would not have it.

"It was awful," she said. "It was the most awful time of my life."

When the nurse brought her supper, she ate it in their company, trying to press various bits upon them. "Wouldn't you like just a little bit of meat?" she would say. "Or at least a carrot?"

They both assured her that they would be able to eat at the party, and she seemed to regret not being able to go. "There'll be a lot of interesting people," she said. "Just about everyone from the British Council."

But when it came near the time for them to leave, all her new-found composure collapsed. She clung to Max and tears ran down her cheeks.

156

"I'll wait in the entrance hall," said Anna. She kissed Mama. "See you in the morning," she said as cheerfully as she could manage. Mama gazed at her distractedly through her tears. "Of course," she murmured. "You'll still be here, won't you, Anna." Then she turned back to Max, and the last thing Anna heard as she left the room was her unhappy voice saying, "Oh, Max – I don't know if I can go on."

Outside, the lights in the corridors were already dimmed down. There was no one about and, although it was not yet nine o'clock, it felt like the middle of the night. In the entrance hall, only a shaded lamp shone on the desk where the porter sat writing figures in a book, and he did not look up when Anna came in. The heating must be turned down as well as the lights, she thought, for she felt suddenly cold.

She found a chair and sat there, listening to the scratching of the porter's pen and thinking about Mama. Mama weeping, Mama saying, "I can't go on," Mama in the blue hat . . .

A car drove past outside, scraping the gravel. The waiting-room chairs threw leaping shadows across the walls, and in the glass kiosk where flowers and chocolates were sold during the day, a tinselly bird on a box of sweets was momentarily picked out and sparkled in the darkness.

And then she suddenly remembered. She remembered the time Mama had cried while wearing her blue hat with the veil. Not gradually, but all at once, completely, as though it had just that minute happened, and her first feeling was one of amazement that she could ever have forgotten.

It had happened – if anything had happened at all – during her first year at art school. Everyone had thought that, once the war was over, things would be better, but for Mama and Papa they had got worse. Papa's health was failing and, since so many young people had returned from the fighting, Mama could no longer get even the third-rate secretarial jobs which had, until then, kept them afloat.

Anna still shared a room with Mama and had felt full of compassion. But she was also doing what she wanted for the first time since she was grown up. She had only three years in which to do it, and she was determined that nothing was going to stop her. She still had long conversations with Papa about painting and writing – things which interested them both. But when Mama started on her money worries and the hopelessness of the future, there was a point beyond which she would not listen. She would nod her head deceitfully and escape into thoughts of her work and her friends, and Mama who always knew, of course, what she was up to, would call her cold and unaffectionate.

And then one day – it must have been a Saturday, because she had been shopping in Putney High Street – this curious thing had happened.

She had just caught a bus home and was still standing on the platform, when she had heard her name called by what seemed to be a disembodied voice. She was tired and nervous after pretending to listen to Mama late into the previous night, and for a moment the sound had really frightened her. Then she had seen Mama's face, white and tense, looking up at her from the pavement as the bus swept by, and she had jumped off at the traffic lights and hurried back to her.

"What is it?" she had asked, and even now she could clearly see Mama standing there, outside Woolworth's, shouting, "I don't want to go on! I can't!"

She had felt angry and helpless, but before she could say anything, Mama had cried, "It didn't work. I really tried and it didn't work."

"What didn't work?" she had asked, and Mama had said, "The Professor's pills." Then she had looked Anna straight in the eye and said, "I took them."

At first, she remembered, she had not known what Mama was talking about. She had just stared at Mama as she stood there in her blue hat with a windowful of Woolworth's Easter chicks behind her. And then, suddenly, she had understood.

The Professor, a friend, had given Papa the pills in 1940, as a last resort in case he and Mama were captured by the Nazis. They were instant poison.

She had stared at Mama in horror and cried, "When did you take them?" and Mama had said, "Last night, when you were asleep. I took one, but nothing happened, and then I took the other, and still nothing happened, and then I thought perhaps there was a delayed effect and I waited, but nothing happened, nothing happened at all!" She had begun to cry, and then she had noticed Anna's horrified face and said, "I took them in the bathroom, so that you wouldn't find me dead in bed."

Anna had suddenly felt very old – perhaps that was when it all began, she thought – and angry that Mama should have made her feel like this, and yet dreadfully, overwhelmingly sorry for her. She had been conscious of the pavement under her feet and of the shoppers pushing past her in and out of Woolworth's, and she had looked at Mama crying with the Easter chicks behind her, and at last she had said, "Well, of course it would have made all the difference to me, finding you dead in the bathroom instead."

Mama had sniffed and said, "I thought perhaps the maid might find me."

"For God's sake," Anna had shouted, "the maid, me, Papa – what difference does it make?" and Mama had said in a small voice, "Well, I knew it would upset you, of course." She had looked so absurd, with her snub nose and her blue hat with the veil, that Anna had suddenly started to laugh. Mama had asked, "Why is that funny?" But then she had laughed as well, and they had both become aware of an icy wind blowing down Putney High Street and had gone inside Woolworth's to get warm.

She could not remember exactly what had

happened after that. They had walked round Woolworth's – she rather thought Mama had bought some mending thread – and they had talked about the extraordinary fact that the Professor's pills had been completely innocuous. ("I might have known they wouldn't work," Mama had said, "I always thought he was a charlatan.") She remembered wondering what the Professor would have done if there had really been a Nazi invasion. Would he then have replaced them with proper ones? But perhaps, said Mama, the pills they had were really effective, only they had lost their strength over the years. From what she could recall of her chemistry lessons at school, she seemed to believe that this was possible.

They had ended up drinking tea at Lyons and, with Mama sitting hale and hearty on the other side of the table, it had seemed as though, after all, nothing had really happened.

And had it? wondered Anna in the half-darkness of the hospital, while the sound of the car slowly faded, someone, somewhere, shut a door, and the porter's pen went on scratching.

There had been so much talk, in those days, of suicide. For Mama, just talking about it might have been a kind of safety valve. Perhaps she never even took the pills, thought Anna, or else she knew all along that they wouldn't work. If Mama had really tried to kill herself, she thought, surely I could not have forgotten. She could not remember ever talking about it to Max or Papa. But perhaps she had just not wanted to think about it, so as to get on with her own life.

She was still trying to work it out, when she jumped at a touch. It was Konrad, reassuringly large and patient.

"Your brother's just coming," he said. "Let's go to this dreadful party, so you can ring up your Richard."

Ken Hathaway lived in an old-fashioned flat full of heavy German furniture. He seemed inordinately pleased to see them and welcomed them with a delighted, rabbity smile.

"So nice to see new faces," he cried. "The old ones do get rather used in such a small community – don't you agree, Konrad?"

There was a large silver bowl containing a pale liquid with bits of fruit afloat in it, and a fair-haired young German was ladling it into glasses.

"German cold punch," said Ken proudly. "Günther's own concoction. God knows what he puts in it."

Judging by the happy sounds of the guests, thought Anna, it was probably plenty.

As Ken was about to sweep them off and introduce them, Konrad put a restraining hand on his arm. "Just before we join the festivities," he said, "do you think Anna could ring her husband in London?"

"Only very quickly," she said.

Ken waved a generous hand. "My dear," he

said, "help yourself. It's in the bedroom. But you'll be lucky if you get through. There've been delays all day – this wretched Suez business, I suppose."

She found the bedroom filled with everybody's coats, and sat on the edge of the bed in a gap between them. The operator took a long time to answer and then gave a disapproving snort when asked for London. "Up to two hours' delay," he said, and was persuaded only with difficulty to book the call.

When she emerged from the bedroom, Konrad and Max had already been absorbed by the party. Konrad was talking to a bald man in a dark suit, and Max had got a middle-aged blonde who was gazing at him with the stunned delight so long familiar to Anna, as though she had just found a lot of gold at the bottom of her handbag. Then Ken bore down on her with a glass and an earnest-looking man who turned out to be some kind of academic.

"I'm interested in medieval history," he shouted over the mixed English and German voices, "though here I'm working on –" But she never discovered what he was working on, for a grey-haired woman next to her gave a little scream.

"Suez! Hungary!" she cried. "What a fuss they make about these things. Here in Berlin we're used to crises. Were you here during the Airlift?"

Her partner, a small clerkish person, had carelessly been elsewhere, and she abandoned him with contempt, but a fat German with glasses smiled his agreement.

"Berlin can take it," he shouted, with difficulty, in English. "Like London, *nicht wahr*, in the bomps?"

Anna could think of nothing to reply to this, so she looked vague and thought of Richard, while the voices rose another decibel.

". . . trigger off World War Three," cried an invisible strategist, and the academic's measured tones rose momentarily above the rest. "One old and one new empire, each clinging to its conquests . . ."

"More punch," said Günther and filled up the glasses.

Someone had closed the bedroom door and she wondered if she would still be able to hear the telephone. Out of the corner of her eye, she could see Ken lead Max away from the blonde who followed him sadly with her eyes, and introduce him to a tall man with a pipe.

"They could take Berlin in ten minutes," said the grey-haired woman, and someone replied, "But the United States of America . . ."

Then Ken was upon her and propelled her to another part of the room, where various people asked after Mama and expressed pleasure at her recovering from pneumonia. Clearly Konrad had done a good job in explaining her illness.

"We really miss her," said an American colonel, meaning it. "In a tight little community like ours . . ." A woman with a fringe said, "She's the best translator we've got," and a girl with freckles and a pony tail said, "Somehow you can always tell when she's *there*."

More punch – Ken pouring this time. A sudden burst of laughter from a group nearby, followed by a ringing sound, so that for a moment she thought it was the telephone, but it was only all of them clinking glasses.

"Excuse me," she said.

She wove her way through the crowd, went into the bedroom and came out again, leaving the door ajar. On her way back she passed Max who had been rejoined by the blonde and several other people and she heard one of them say admiringly, "Really? To Athens? Tonight?" Konrad saw her and waved, and she was just wondering whether to fight her way through to him, when she heard herself being addressed in German and found Günther beside her.

"I must tell you," he said. "I've read your father's works."

"Really?" She wondered what on earth was coming.

"Yes." He gazed at her ardently over the half-empty jug of punch. "I think they're –" He searched for the words. "Terribly relevant," he managed at last, triumphantly.

"Do you?" His fresh face shone under the blond hair. He couldn't be more than eighteen, she decided. "I'm so glad you liked them."

He put down the jug, so as to concentrate better. "I think everyone should read them," he said.

She was touched. "Did you like the poems?" she said.

"The poems? Oh yes, the poems too. But his political awareness at that time – that's what I really find incredible."

"Well, it was rather forced upon him," said Anna. "By circumstances. His real loves were the theatre and travel –" but he was not listening. In his excitement he had advanced upon her and she found herself wedged in between him and the table holding the jug.

"Terrible mistakes have been made," cried Günther. "Our parents made them, to Germany's shame, and it is up to my generation to put them right." He brought his hand down sharply on the table and the jug trembled.

She looked for a way of escape but there was none.

"How?" she asked. If my call comes through now, she thought, I'll have to dive through under the table.

"Very simple," said Günther confidentially. "We shall discuss. My comrades and I discuss everything."

"Do you?"

He nodded and smiled. "Every Tuesday. Yesterday we discussed the Nazi ethic, and next week we shall discuss the persecution of the Jews."

"Really," she said. "On Tuesday."

He beamed at her. "Would you like to come?"

At that moment, to her relief, she saw Hildy Goldblatt, only a little way behind him, gazing round the room. She caught her eye and waved, and Hildy waved back and moved towards her.

"Excuse me," she said, as Hildy reached them, and he stepped aside reluctantly.

"My dear," said Hildy after a brief nod at him, "isn't this dreadful? I have seen some food on a table next door. Let's go and talk quietly in there."

Anna followed her, making sure that all doors remained open so that she could hear the telephone, and they sat down near the depleted buffet.

"Well then," said Hildy, tucking into some bread and sausage, "your Mama is quite better. I told you everything would be all right. But your husband must be worried about you: the Suez business now as well as Hungary. When are you going home?"

She looked at Hildy, her frizzy hair sticking out untidily from her clever, affectionate face, and wondered how much she had guessed.

"I don't know," she said carefully. "I'm waiting for a call from him now."

Hildy nodded and chewed.

"I want to go home," said Anna. "Only Max has to leave tonight, and I'm not sure . . ."

"If your Mama can manage without both of you."

"Yes."

"Yes," Hildy polished off the sausage with one bite. "I can't stay long," she said. "My Erwin is not well – something with his stomach. In any case, one should never give advice. But if it's any use –" She hesitated. "It's only what I think," she said. "But I think that Konrad . . . will do what needs to be done. I think – I think one can trust him. You understand what I mean?"

"Yes," said Anna.

"He is a kind man. And anyway," said Hildy, "you should be home with your husband now. I know we have had a lot of frights and always, at the last minute, the politicians draw back, but at such times it is no good for people to be apart." She heaved herself out of the chair. "I really must go. My poor Erwin. He has vomited, you know, and that is something which, for him, is not at all normal."

As they entered the other room, the party appeared to have quietened down. A number of guests must have left, and the rest were sitting rather than standing, some of them on the floor, and talking in undertones.

"Always the same faces," said Hildy. "What can they find to talk about?"

Konrad hurried towards them. "Are you going, Hildy? We ought to go as well, to get Max to the airport."

"But I'm still waiting for my call from Richard," said Anna, and at that moment the telephone rang. She cried, "That'll be him," embraced Hildy quickly, and ran to the bedroom. Someone had closed the door again. She threw it open and found herself looking straight at a girl with her dress unzipped and pulled halfway down off her shoulders. Immediately behind her, a man with a handlebar moustache was making great play of adjusting his tie over his unbuttoned shirt. The telephone was still ringing.

"Excuse me," she said, edging past both of them, and answered it.

At first there seemed to be no one there, then there was a buzzing sound and an unidentifiable voice saying something a long way off.

The man and the girl – her dress now pulled up again – were watching her uncertainly.

"Hullo?" she said. "Hullo?"

The voice faded, but the buzzing continued.

"Hullo," she said more loudly. "Hullo. Hullo. Hullo."

Nothing happened, but the handlebar moustache suddenly appeared very close to her face, exuding alcoholic fumes.

"Just-look-ing-for-her-hand-bag," its owner explained, pronouncing each syllable with great care and lifting up one of the coats to show what he meant.

She nodded impatiently and waved him away.

"Hullo?" she shouted into the telephone. "Hullo? Richard, is that you?"

Somewhere infinitely far away, she heard Richard's voice. "Hullo, love. Are you all right?" and at once all her anxieties and tensions melted away.

"Yes," she shouted. "Are you?"

He said something she could not catch, and she shouted, "Mama is out of danger."

Richard's voice suddenly came through loud and clear.

"What?" he said.

"Mama is out of danger. She's going to be all right."

"Oh, I'm glad."

Out of the corner of her eye, she could see the girl self-consciously straightening her hair and leaving the room, followed by the man. Thank God, she thought.

"Richard, it's lovely to hear you."

"And you. When are you coming home?"

"Well, what do you think? What do you think about this Suez business?"

"It's difficult to –" The buzzing began again and drowned the rest of his words.

"I can't hear you," she cried.

He repeated whatever he had said – she could tell he must be shouting – but all she could catch were the words "if possible".

"Do you want me to come home? Richard? Would you like me to come home straight away?" She was shouting at the top of her voice.

There was a little click. The buzzing stopped, and a German operator said loudly and clearly, "*Charlottenburg* exchange. Can I help you?"

"You cut me off!" she shouted. "I was talking to London and you cut me off. Please reconnect me at once."

"I'm sorry," said the voice. "There is a three hour delay to London and we are accepting no more calls."

"But I was talking to them. I was talking to them, and you cut me off in the middle."

"I'm sorry, but there is nothing I can do."

"Please!" cried Anna. "I've waited all day for this call. It's really important."

But of course it was no use.

After she had put down the receiver, she stayed sitting among the coats for a moment, fighting an overwhelming urge to break something, to be sick, to walk straight out and catch the next plane to London. Then she stood up and went back to the party.

"All right?" said Konrad. He was waiting for her with Max's briefcase in his hand. "Come on, Max," he called before she could answer. "We really must go."

Max was having some difficulty in disentangling the blonde who appeared to be offering to come to Athens with him. Behind him, someone had rolled back the carpet and a number of people, mostly middle-aged, were dancing to the radio.

"Coming," said Max, managing to ditch the blonde at last. Ken handed them their coats and they hurried towards the door. "So sorry you have to leave . . . regards to your Mama . . ." Teeth bared in smiles, handshakes, *auf Wiedersehens*, and then they were outside in the dark, and Konrad was driving very fast towards Tempelhof.

"Did you get Richard?" asked Max, turning back in his seat, while shadows of trees and lamp posts raced across them.

She shook her head. "I couldn't hear him, and

then we were cut off." If I'm not careful, she thought, I'm going to weep all over the car.

He made a face. "Don't worry. Any sign of trouble and you go straight home. All right?"

"All right."

Konrad was leaning forward over the steering wheel, and the car was tearing along through the night. "I hope we'll make it," he said without taking his eyes off the road.

Max glanced at his watch. "Christ," he said. "I didn't know it was so late." He began to drum with his fingers and stare tensely into the darkness ahead.

She sat in the back, her coat wrapped round her for warmth, feeling alone. Her chin tucked into her collar, her hands thrust deep into her pockets, she tried to think of nothing. Then she felt something under her fingers, something thin and rustly – a piece of paper. She pulled it out and, by holding it very close to her eyes, could just distinguish the word "Heals" printed across the top. It must be the bill for the dining-room rug.

It seemed like something from another world, from the infinitely distant past which had gone and would never come again. She clutched it in her cold hand and suddenly felt desperate. I've got no business to be here, she thought, surrounded by Russians when there might be a war. I don't belong here. I should be home with Richard. Suppose I never get home? Suppose I never see him again? She stared at the dark, unfamiliar landscape racing past the window and thought in terror, I might be here for ever.

At last there were lights. The car swerved and braked.

"See you in London, little man," said Max and scrambled out before it had properly stopped.

She watched him run to the airport entrance, his shadow leaping wildly beside him. There was a dazzle of light as he opened the door, and then he was gone.

"I think he'll just catch it," said Konrad.

They waited in case he didn't and wanted to come back, but nothing happened. The door remained closed. After what seemed like a long time, Anna climbed into the front seat and they drove slowly back to the centre of town. It was one o'clock in the morning and very cold.

"I'm sorry you couldn't speak to Richard," said Konrad after a few kilometres.

She was too depressed to do anything but nod. It suddenly seemed a familiar feeling. Of course, she thought. All those times in Putney when Max had gone back to the Air Force or to Cambridge. This was how she had felt then. It did not seem so very long ago. Back with Mama, she thought. Trapped. She could almost sense the Russians all around.

"I entirely agree with Max, you know," said Konrad. "At the first hint of trouble, you get on a plane to London."

She could see his face, greenish-grey in the glimmer from the dashboard. Behind it, indistinct dark shapes fled through his reflection in the glass.

"I wish –" she said.

"That you were at home with Richard instead of driving round Berlin in the early hours of the morning."

"Not just that. I wish Mama lived in a house. I wish she liked cooking and made large meals which nobody could eat, and fussed about people's appetites and the cleaning." For a moment she could almost persuade herself that it was possible.

"Where?" said Konrad.

"Somewhere." She knew it was nonsense. "Not in Berlin."

They were off the main road now, into lamplit side streets – the beginning of the suburbs.

"She's never been keen on domesticity," said Konrad. He added loyally, "Thank God."

"Well, if she could just take life as it comes. Make the most of what there is, even if it isn't perfect. Rather than this awful romanticism, this rejection of everything that isn't exactly as she's dreamed it. After all, there are other ways of solving one's problems than by committing suicide."

His eyes left the road for a moment and flickered towards her. "Aren't you being rather hard on her?"

"I don't think so. After all, I've lived with her a lot longer than you have." The anger and frustrations of the day suddenly boiled over inside her. "You don't know what it was like," she said, and was surprised how loud her voice sounded.

They had reached a familiar arrangement of shops and houses. The car turned a corner, then another, and there was the street with her hotel.

"I think I can imagine," he said. "She's often told me about it. The worst time of her life, as she calls it. I know how she talks, but it must have been quite difficult for her as well as you."

He stopped the car outside the hotel, switched off the engine, and they sat for a moment without talking. In the silence she could hear a faint, distant tremor. Thunder, she thought, and her stomach contracted.

"That's one of the things I feel worst about," he said.

"What?"

He hesitated. "Well, look at me. I'm not exactly a film star. With my paunch and my slipped disk and my face like the back of a bus. Hardly the sort of man for whom women commit suicide. And yet, somehow, I've driven your mother . . ."

The thunder was getting closer. She could see the drawn expression on his face, very pale in the light of a street lamp.

". . . I've driven her to do something which, even during the worst period of her life, she was never tempted to do."

"How do you know?"

"That I drove her to it?"

"No." Part of her was too angry to think, but another part knew exactly what she was saying. "That she was never tempted to do it before."

He stared at her in the dimness of the car, and she stared back. There was another rumble of thunder – strange in November, she thought – and then she suddenly realized that it was not thunder at all.

"Listen!" She could hardly get it out. "It's gunfire."

His mind was still on what she had been saying, and he did not seem to understand.

"It's the Russians!" For a moment it was like water closing over her head. Then she felt quite calm. Goodbye, she thought. Goodbye, Richard. Goodbye, everything she had ever wanted to do. Mama and Berlin for always. It had caught up with her at last, as she had always known it would.

"The Russians?" said Konrad, very surprised.

She was struggling with the window and finally got it open. "Can't you hear it?"

"My dear," he said, "my dear, it's nothing, you mustn't be so frightened. That's not the Russians, it's the Americans."

"The Americans?"

He nodded. "Artillery practice. Every other Thursday – though usually not quite so early in the morning."

"The Americans." She couldn't have breathed for a while, for she felt as though her lungs had stuck together. Now she opened her mouth, and a lot of air rushed in. "I'm sorry," she said and felt herself blush. "I don't normally get so panicked."

"It was perfectly natural." His face was even more drawn than before. "I ought to have warned you. But living here, one forgets."

"Anyway, I'm all right now. I'd better go to bed." She made to get out, but he put out his hand.

"I've been thinking," he said.

"What?"

"Various things. First of all, I think you should go home."

Her heart leapt. "But what about Mama?"

"*Nu,* she is no longer seriously ill. Of course I should have been glad of your support a little longer, but I had not realized how difficult all this has been for you. Could you still stay over tomorrow?"

"Well, of course."

"Good. Then we will book you a flight for Friday, and I'll send a cable to Richard that you're coming."

Suddenly she no longer felt cold. She could feel the blood rushing into her toes and fingers, warming them. Her whole body was aglow with relief, and she looked at Konrad's pale, heavy face, filled with an almost physical affection for him.

"Are you sure?" she asked, knowing that it was quite safe to do so.

"Absolutely."

The day after tomorrow, she thought. Tomorrow, really, for they were already well into Thursday. Then she realized that Konrad was still talking.

"I hope you don't mind my asking," he said. "But you understand that it's important for me to know. After all, I am very much concerned."

To know what?

He hesitated how best to put it. "Has your mother ever, previously . . . Did she ever, before, try to kill herself?"

What did it matter, now that she was going home? She wished she had never brought it up. "I don't know," she said. "I really don't."

"But you were saying earlier –"

She could simply deny it, she thought, but he was looking at her with his worried eyes, blaming himself. She did not want him to feel so guilty.

"There was something," she said slowly at last. "But I don't honestly think it was very serious. In fact I'd forgotten all about it until today."

"What happened?"

So, as lightly as possible, she told him about the Professor's pills. "I think she knew they wouldn't work," she said. "I think she just had to do something, and so she pretended. After all, if she'd really tried to kill herself, I wouldn't have forgotten."

"Wouldn't you?"

"Well, of course not. It would have been too awful to forget."

"Or too awful to remember."

Nonsense, she thought.

"Look," he said, "I've seen as many bad psychological thrillers as you have. I have no wish to act like an amateur – headshrinker, isn't it called? But those pills were supposed to be poison, and your mother did take them."

"I'm not even sure of that."

"I think she took them," said Konrad.

She had wanted him to feel less guilty, but he seemed almost exultant. There was an edge to his voice which she had not heard before, and she suddenly wondered what on earth she had done.

Thursday

During what was left of the night, she slept only fitfully. She dreamed endlessly of Mama – Mama wandering on a mountainside, in the streets, through the rooms of an ever-expanding house, and always searching for Konrad. Sometimes she found him and sometimes she only glimpsed him for a moment before he disappeared. Once Anna found him for her, and Mama hugged her on the beach and laughed delightedly with the sun on the sand behind her. Another time he slipped away from them in Woolworth's while Anna was buying Mama a hat.

She woke uneasy and depressed, much later than usual, and found the breakfast room deserted, with only a few dirty cups and plates still cluttered on the tables. The proprietress, engaged half-heartedly in clearing them away, stopped at the sight of her.

"Have you heard?" she said. "The Russians are leaving Budapest." As Anna looked at her, uncomprehending, she repeated it in her thick Berlin accent. "*Sie gehen*," she said. "*Die Russen gehen*," and produced a newspaper to prove it.

Anna read it while the woman scurried about, clattering the used crockery and turning the stained table cloths. Incredibly, it was true. She could hardly believe it. Why? she wondered. The West must have acted. A secret message from the White House, leaving no room for doubt. All the free countries together, united as they had never been against the Nazis until it was too late. She looked for news of Suez, but only found a small paragraph. Nothing much seemed to be happening there.

"They'll be happy today in Budapest," said the woman, putting down some coffee and rolls before her. "Dancing in the streets, it said on the radio. And they've pulled down a great statue of Stalin – whatever will they do with it, do you suppose? And they're going to change everything and have things just the way they want them."

Anna drank her coffee and felt suddenly better. It was all going to be all right. Unlike the Nazis, the Russians were not going to get away with it. Mama was alive and almost well again. She was going home – Konrad had said so. Just as long as nothing happens to stop it, she thought.

"I can just imagine how they're feeling in Hungary," said the woman, lingering by the table with the empty tray in her hands. "When I think of what the Russians did here . . ." And she embarked on a long rambling story about a soldier who had fired six shots into a stone gnome in her front garden. "And he was shouting, 'Nazi! Nazi!' all the time," she said in a shocked voice. "After all, the gnome was not a Nazi." After a moment's thought she added, "And nor, of course, was I."

Anna struggled to keep a straight face and stuffed herself with the rolls and butter. She did not want to be late for her visit to Mama, especially if she were leaving the following day. Even so, she missed her usual bus and had to wait ten minutes for the next.

It was cold, with dark, drifting clouds which every so often erupted into drizzle, and when at last she arrived at the hospital, the warmth of the entrance hall enveloped her like a cocoon. The receptionist smiled at her – I'm beginning to belong to the place, she thought – and Mama's little room, with the rain spitting on the double windows and the radiator blasting away, was welcoming and snug.

"Hullo, Mama," she said. "Isn't it good about Hungary?"

"Incredible," said Mama.

She was looking much brighter, sitting up in bed in a fresh nightie, with a newspaper beside her, and began at once to ask about the party and about Max's departure. "So Konrad drove him straight from the party to the airport," she said when Anna had described it all. It was the bit that pleased her most.

There were new flowers on her table, as well as a lavish box of chocolates from her office and a coloured card with "Get well soon, honey" on it and a lot of signatures. Konrad had rung up earlier, while she was in her bath, but had left a message that he would ring again. She leaned back into the pillows, relaxed for the first time since she had got better.

"By the way," she said in the warm, no-nonsense voice which Anna remembered so clearly from her childhood, "the nurse told me what you did when I was in a coma – about you being here so much of the time and sitting on my bed and calling me. I'm sorry, I didn't know. One doesn't remember, you see." She added with curious formality. "She says you may have saved my life. Thank you."

Anna found herself unexpectedly touched. She cast about for something to answer, but could think of nothing adequate so she grinned and said, as Max might have done, "That's all right, Mama – any time," and Mama giggled and said, "You're dreadful – you're just as bad as your brother," which, coming from Mama, she supposed was the nicest thing she could have said.

She looked so much more like herself that she decided to broach the question of leaving.

"Mama," she said, "I've been here nearly a week. I'd really like to go home. Do you think, if I could get a flight tomorrow, you'd be all right?"

She was about to add various qualifications about keeping in touch and not going unless Mama was absolutely sure, when Mama said, in the same sensible voice, "I'm much better now, and after all it's only ten days till I go away with Konrad. I think I'll be all right." Then she said, "But I'll miss you," and touched Anna's hand gently with her fingers. "I've hardly talked to you."

"You were talking to Max."

"I know," said Mama. "But I see him so seldom." She said again, "I'll miss you."

"I'll write every day," said Anna. She had decided this in advance. "Even if it isn't very interesting. So that if you're feeling low or Konrad is busy or anything, at least you'll know that *something* will happen."

"That'll be nice," said Mama. She thought for a moment. Then she said, "I'm sorry – I realize now that all this has been a lot of trouble to everyone, but, you know, I still can't see any reason why I shouldn't have done it."

Anna's heart sank.

"For God's sake, Mama –"

"No, listen, let's not pretend. Let's talk about this honestly." Mama was very serious. "I'm fifty-six, and I'm alone. I've done all the things I had to do. I brought you and Max up and got you through the emigration. I looked after Papa and I've got his books republished, which I promised him I'd do. Nobody needs me any longer. Why shouldn't I die if I want to?"

"Of course we need you," said Anna, but Mama gestured impatiently.

"I said, let's be honest. I don't say that you wouldn't be pleased to see me occasionally, say at

Christmas or something, but you don't *need* me." She looked at Anna challengingly. "Tell me," she said. "Tell me honestly, what difference would it have made if I had died?"

Anna knew at once what difference it would have made. She would have blamed herself for the rest of her life for not having, somehow, given Mama enough reason to go on living. But you couldn't ask people to stay alive just to stop you feeling guilty.

"If you had died," she said after a moment, "I would have been the child of two suicides."

Mama disposed of that in a flash. "Nonsense," she said. "Papa's suicide didn't count." She glared at Anna, daring her to disagree.

"One suicide, then," said Anna, feeling ridiculous.

They stared at each other, and then Mama began to giggle.

"Honestly," she said, "can you imagine anyone else having a conversation like this?"

"Not really," said Anna, and somehow they were back in Putney, in Bloomsbury, in the cramped flat in Paris, in the Swiss village inn – a close, close family surrounded by people different from themselves. As the familiar sensation enveloped her, she suddenly knew what to say.

"I'll tell you what difference it would have made," she said. "Though you may not think it enough of a reason. But whenever anything happens to me, anything good like a new job or even something quite small like a party or buying a new dress, my first thought is always, I must tell Mama. I know I don't always do it. I don't always write, and when we meet I've maybe forgotten. But I always think it. And if you were dead, I wouldn't be able to think it any more, and then the thing that happened, whatever it was, wouldn't be nearly as good."

She looked at Mama expectantly.

"That's very sweet of you," said Mama. "But it's not a reason to go on living." Then she sniffed, and her eyes were suddenly wet. "But it's very sweet of you, just the same," she said.

After this neither of them knew quite what to do, until Mama grabbed hold of the box on the table and said, "Would you like a chocolate?"

Anna made a great fuss of choosing one, and Mama told her, as she had often told her before, about a governess she had had as a child, who, for reasons of daintiness, had insisted on always eating chocolates in one bite. "So you never found out what was inside them," said Mama indignantly, as always when she remembered the story.

They were just choosing another chocolate each when the telephone rang on the bedside table.

"That'll be Konrad," said Mama, and as she put the receiver to her ear, Anna could hear him saying, "Good morning, ma'am."

"Give him my regards," she said, and went over to the window, so as not to look as though she were listening.

It was still raining outside, and she could see the tops of the trees, now almost bare, blowing in the wind. Someone had tried to sweep the carefully laid out paths, but already the leaves were drifting back across them from the grass.

"Oh yes, I'm much better," said Mama behind her, and went on to talk about what she had eaten and what the doctor had said. Some birds – sparrows, she thought – had found an old piece of bread and were pecking at it, jostling each other and pushing each other away. She could see their feathers glistening with the rain, but they did not seem to mind.

"Have you fixed up about your leave?" said Mama. "Because, if we're going to book the hotel –"

The piece of bread, pecked by one of the birds, rose up into the air to land a foot or so away, and all the rest half-hopped, half-flew to follow it.

"What do you mean?" Mama's voice suddenly sounded different. "What do you mean, see what happens in the office first?"

Anna tried, without success, to keep her mind on the sparrows who had now pulled the bread in half.

"But you said – you promised!" Mama's voice was rising. Stealing a glance at her, Anna could see that her face was flushed and upset.

"Well, I've been ill as well. Don't I deserve some consideration? For heaven's sake, Konrad, what do you think I'm going to do?"

Oh God, thought Anna. She took a step towards Mama with some idea of offering support, but at the sight of her face, closed to everything except the crackle from the telephone, abandoned it.

"Yes, I know the work is important, but this is the one thing that's kept me going. Surely Erwin could manage. Why are you suddenly so concerned for him?" Mama was biting back her tears, and her voice was almost out of control, "Well, how do you know it is serious? Are you sure it's really Erwin you're worried about and not someone quite different?" The telephone crackled, and she shouted, "No, I don't believe you. I don't know what to believe. For all I know, she's there with you now, or listening on the extension."

"Mama –" said Anna, but there was no stopping her.

"I'm not hysterical," yelled Mama. "I've been ill, and I nearly died, and I wish to God I had." She was crying now, and angrily wiping the tears away with her hand. "I wanted to die. You know I wanted to die. Why on earth didn't you let me?"

The telephone spat, and her face suddenly went rigid.

"What do you mean?" she cried. "Konrad, what do you mean?"

But he had rung off.

Anna went over to the bed and sat cautiously on the edge. "What's happened?" she said in as matter of fact a voice as she could manage. She suddenly felt very tired.

Mama took a trembling breath. "He hasn't applied for leave," she brought out at last. "He doesn't know if he can get away." She turned her head away. "I always knew," she said indistinctly into the sheets. "I always knew it was no good – that it could never come right."

"Mama," said Anna, "what exactly did he say?"

Mama looked at her with her hurt blue eyes. "I don't know," she said. "Something about Erwin being ill. And then, at the end –"

"Erwin *is* ill," said Anna. "He was sick yesterday. Hildy told me." But Mama was not listening.

"He said something about it not being the first time. I said I wanted to die, and he said – I couldn't quite catch it, but I'm sure he said, 'Well, it isn't the first time, is it?'" She stared at Anna, her face working nervously. "Why on earth should he say that?"

Anna felt as though a huge stone were rolling slowly towards her and there was no way of escape. "I don't know," she said. "Perhaps he was just upset."

"It didn't sound like that."

"Oh, God, Mama, how do I know what he meant?" She suddenly wanted nothing further to do with it, not with Mama, not with Konrad, not with any of them. "It's not my business," she shouted. "I came here because you were ill, and I've done my best to make you better. I can't do anything more. It's too complicated for me. I can't tell you how to run your life."

"Nobody asked you to." Mama was glaring at her and she glared back for a moment, but could not keep it up. "What's the matter with you?" asked Mama.

"Nothing," she said, and then, to her relief, there was a knock at the door and a nurse came in.

"Excuse me," she said. (It was the friendly one.) "I'd like just to take a peep at your telephone."

They both watched her walk across to the bedside table, and heard the tiny ping as she adjusted the receiver on its support. "There,' she said. "The cord had caught under it." She smiled at Mama. "Dr Rabin telephoned for you. We couldn't get through to your room, so he left a message with the switchboard. He's on his way to see you."

"Now?" said Mama.

"That's right. I told him he mustn't stay long because it's nearly time for your lunch, and then you must have your rest. All right?"

"Yes," said Mama, looking confused. As soon as the nurse had gone, she turned to Anna and said, "It's no distance in the car. He'll be here in a moment."

"I'll go."

"Could you just – I'd like to wash my face."

"Of course."

She climbed out of bed, looking as she had looked in the mornings in Putney, the pink night-dress clinging to her middle-aged legs (they were short and chubby like Anna's), the childlike eyes tense. While she poured water on her face with her hands and nervously combed her crisp grey hair,

Anna straightened the sheets. Then she helped Mama back into bed and tucked the bedclothes round her.

"All right?" she said. "You look very nice."

Mama bit her lip and nodded.

"I'm sure it'll all be fine." She tried to think of something else to say – something that would give Mama courage, that would make her say all the right things to Konrad and at the same time, somehow, exonerate herself – but there was nothing.

"See you later," she said. Then she smiled hypocritically and left.

As she passed through the entrance hall, she saw Konrad coming up the steps outside. For a moment she thought of intercepting him – "Please don't tell Mama that I told you . . ." But what was the use? Instead, she went and stood behind a group of people buying flowers at the kiosk, and he stumped past with his stick without seeing her. She did not dare look up until after he had passed. From the back, with his thinning hair disarranged by the wind, he looked old – too old, she thought, to be involved in a love affair, let alone a triangular one.

Outside, the cold stung her face and she walked as fast as she could down the wide, windswept road. It was no longer raining, but the temperature must have dropped several degrees, for her coat seemed suddenly too thin. The wind blew right through it, round her shoulders and up her sleeves, and since she had no idea, in any case, where she was going, she turned down a side street to escape from it.

Here it was more sheltered, and she slowed down a little, though still keeping her mind on her surroundings and on putting one foot in front of the other. She had no wish to think of Mama's room in the hospital, or of what she and Konrad might now be saying to each other.

"I can't cope with all that," she said aloud.

There was no one to hear her except a dog loitering in the gutter. No people. They were all at work, she supposed, rebuilding Germany. She passed only two or three cars, a boy on a bicycle and an old man swathed in jackets and scarves, snipping away in one of the overgrown gardens which edged the pavement.

What shall I do? she thought, sinking her chin into her collar against the cold. She couldn't go on walking about for ever. Sooner or later she would have to go back to Mama – and what would happen then? I'll have to find out from Konrad what he said to her, she thought, but her heart sank at the prospect.

At the end of the street, the view became more open. A main road led to a square with shops and buses and a taxi rank. *Roseneck* said a sign, to her surprise. When she was small, she had come here once a week for her dancing class. She had come on the tram, the fare money tucked inside her glove, and when the conductor called out the stop, she had jumped off and run across – where?

The trams were gone, the square had been

rebuilt, and she recognized nothing. She stood disconsolately in the icy wind, trying to work out where the tram stop would have been, so as not to think, instead, how Mama was probably feeling about her at this moment, but it was no use. It's all gone wrong, she thought, meaning both the business with Mama and her unrecognizable surroundings. She longed for somewhere familiar and reassuring. A sign in the road said, *Richtung Grunewald*, and she suddenly knew what she wanted to do.

It felt strange, giving the taxi driver the old address, and she half-expected him to look surprised. But he only repeated, "number ten," and drove off.

Hagen Strasse, where buses now ran instead of trams, *Königsallee*, with the wind bending branches and tearing through the awnings outside the shops. Turn right into the tree-lined side street, and there they were. It had taken no time at all.

"That's the house," said the driver, as she lingered on the pavement. He seemed anxious to see her actually go in, and only left her there reluctantly. She watched him drive away and disappear around the corner. Then she walked a few steps along – there was nobody about. She found a tree to lean against and stared across at the house, waiting for some kind of emotion.

The house stared back at her. It looked like anywhere else, and she felt put out. There are the steps I used to run up, she told herself. That's where the currant bushes used to be. That is the slope where Max taught me to ride his bicycle.

Nothing. The house stood there like any other. There was a crack in one of the windows, some yellow chrysanthemums were shivering in a flower bed, and a dog was barking shrilly somewhere inside.

But I remembered it all the other day, she thought. She wanted to feel again as she had felt then, to sense with the same ghostly clarity what it had been like to be small, to speak only German and to feel utterly secure in the knowledge of Mama's existence. It seemed to her that if only she could do this, everything would come right. Everything between Mama and herself would be the same as before.

I wore brown lace-up boots, she thought. I had a satchel on my back and I used to run up those steps after school and shout, *"Ist Mami da?"*

"Ist Mami da?" she said aloud.

It sounded merely silly.

On the other side of the road a woman had come out of a house with a shopping bag and was staring across at her. She began to walk slowly down the street. The house next door had been completely rebuilt. Funny, she thought, that she hadn't noticed it the other day. The one beyond that she could not remember at all. Then she came to the corner and stopped again.

At least this still looked the same. There were the rowan trees, now quite bare, and there was the place where the sandbox had been. There was even the lamp post, unnoticed by her before, which Max had once climbed in a game of pirates. She stood looking at it all for a long time. Someone had played here once, she thought, but it did not feel as though it had been her.

As last she became aware of the wind in her back and her feet which were almost frozen. Well, that's over, she thought without knowing exactly what she meant by it. She turned and walked briskly back up the street, a young Englishwoman in a thin tweed coat. It was really cold, as though it might be going to snow. In the *Königsallee* she found a cruising taxi, and asked the driver to take her to Konrad's office.

J.R.S.O. – the Jewish Restitution Successor Office – was housed in a brand-new building not far from the *Kurfürsten Damm*. There were two receptionists, one American and one German, presiding over a mass of forms and pamphlets which explained how to claim restitution for anything of which you might have been robbed by the Nazis, including your nearest and dearest. A few people sat round the walls, waiting for appointments. There was a plan showing the various departments, and arrows pointing the way to go.

She noticed that the mention of Konrad's name was received with respect, and it was not until she was actually going up in the lift that she remembered about his secretary. Christ, she thought, I suppose she'll be there. What on earth will she say? Somehow, she imagined a whole gaggle of girls – I might not even know which one it is, she thought – but when she opened the door to his outer office, there was only one. She was sitting behind a typewriter, talking to a man in a shabby coat, and seemed relieved at the interruption.

"*Guten Tag*," she said with the formal bow of the head that even women practised in Germany. "Can I help you?"

She was only a few years older than herself, thin, with a slightly spinsterish quality, her face plain but not unpleasant. Was this Mama's deadly rival? Anna introduced herself, and it was clear at once that she was. The girl tensed up and said stiffly, "I believe I spoke to you the other day on the telephone." Then she said, "I am glad that your mother is better," and added, "it has all been a great worry to Dr Rabin."

It appeared that Konrad was not yet back.

"He had to go out unexpectedly to attend a meeting," said the girl, apparently believing it, and Anna settled down uncomfortably to wait, while the girl went back to the old man in the coat.

She had never been in Konrad's office before, and while the man mumbled what sounded like a long list of names, she took in the filing cabinets covering the walls to the ceiling – Abrahams, Cohen, Levy, Zuckerman, read the labels on the drawers – the piles of letters on the girl's desk, the sound of typing through a half-open door.

"I know," said the girl in her slight Berlin accent. "But there is really no need. You gave Dr Rabin all this information earlier this morning."

The old man seemed troubled but insistent. He had a big brown envelope and kept putting a shaky hand inside it to feel for something.

"It's the spirit, you see," he said. "The names – well, they're just names, aren't they? Name, age, last-known address – I thought they ought to see . . ." He lost touch with what he was saying, and Anna saw that his hand with its bony knuckles and wrinkled skin now held a sheaf of ancient photographs.

"It's the faces," he said. "You can't understand without the faces." He suddenly put the photographs on the desk in an untidy spread, disarranging a pencil and some papers. The girl drew back slightly.

"My cousin Samuel," he said, pointing. "He was an electrician with the Post Office. Age 36. Last-known address Treblinka. My brother-in-law Arnold, 32. My young niece Miriamne and her brother Alfred –"

"I know, Herr Birnbaum." The girl was clearly put out. "But you see, it isn't necessary. As long as we have the information on the forms, there is no problem about compensation." Her hand moved towards the photographs, wishing to return them to him, but did not quite dare. "We have all the facts we require," she said. "The matter is being dealt with."

Evidently she liked things tidy.

The old man looked at her with his tired eyes. "The gentleman I saw this morning –"

"He's not here," said the girl, but he went straight on talking.

"I think he understood. Please –" He touched one of the pictures with his hand – "I should like him to see."

The girl hesitated. Then, perhaps because she remembered Anna's presence, she gathered them up in a pile. "I'll put them on his desk," she said.

He watched her while she opened the door to the inner office and put them inside. "It really isn't necessary," she could not help saying when she returned. You could see it had upset her. But the old man's face had spread into a quavering smile.

"Thank you," he said. "I shall be easier now." He still seemed to feel that he had not properly explained. "It seems the least you can do," he murmured, "that they should be seen." Then he clutched the empty envelope to his coat and shuffled out of the door.

The girl glanced at Anna after he had gone. "He was here for an hour this morning, talking to Dr Rabin," she said, perhaps fearing that Anna had thought her impatient. "And it isn't even Dr Rabin's job. There is a special department to deal with people like him, but he was so insistent . . ." She adjusted her hair in its neat bun which did not need adjusting. "Dr Rabin always helps people," she said. "But they wear him out."

"He's a very kind man," said Anna.

The girl lit up at once. "Oh, he is," she said. "He certainly is." She was clearly bursting with examples of Konrad's kindness but, realizing that Anna was hardly a suitable confidante, picked up some papers on her desk. "If you'll excuse me, I'll get on with my work." She put a sheet into her typewriter and began to type.

Anna watched her surreptitiously – the broad, competent hands moving efficiently across the keys (Mama could never type like that, she thought) the tidy blouse, the earnest, dutiful expression. She reminded her of someone, but she could not think who. It was hard to think of her as a rival to Mama, and yet, she thought, if one were very tired . . .

"Dr Rabin may have gone straight out to lunch," said the girl. "Would you rather come back later?"

But before Anna could answer, the door opened and Konrad stumped in. He looked startled at the sight of her, but quickly recovered his balance.

"I'm glad you've come," he said in what she supposed must be his official voice. "I wanted to speak to you." He added, "I see you've met my secretary, Ilse."

Ilse was already disposing of his coat and stick. "Did you have an interesting meeting?" she asked, as though it really mattered to her.

He avoided Anna's eye. "Quite interesting," he said, and plunged quickly into the list of messages which she had noted down for him. He sighed at her account of Birnbaum and his photographs. "All right," he said. "I'll think of something to do with them." Then he looked at his watch. "Time you went for your lunch. And perhaps you'd ask them to send us up some sandwiches. Oh, and Ilse, afterwards you might like to have a word with Schmidt of Welfare. I met him in the lift just now, and I was talking to him about the arrangements for your mother –"

Anna did not listen to the details, but whatever arrangements Konrad had suggested, they were obviously very welcome.

He waved Ilse's thanks aside. "Off you go," he said. "And don't forget the sandwiches."

She paused for a moment at the door. "Ham?" she said, blushing a little and smiling. It was clearly a joke between them. He did not catch on for a moment. Then he laughed loudly. "That's right," he said, "ham," and she went.

Once in his office, he waved Anna into a chair and sank into his own with a sigh. "I'm sorry," he said. "It's been a difficult morning. As you can imagine." He absently fingered the photographs on his desk. "You needn't worry about your mother," he said. "I've calmed her down. I've told her that, whatever happens, I'll take her away for a short holiday within a fortnight. She was quite happy with that."

She felt a great sense of relief. "What about Erwin's illness?" she asked.

"Oh –" He gestured impatiently. "Hildy rang me this morning in a great state. It seems they had to call the doctor last night, and he mentioned that it could be hepatitis. It probably isn't. Erwin sounds better already. But of course I'll have to cope with his work, and Ilse threw a small fit – about that and other things – and then poor little Birnbaum . . . I'm afraid it all got on top of me." He had picked up one of the photographs and showed it to her. A small, dark-eyed face, faded and blurred. "'Rachel Birnbaum, aged six.' No wonder he's a little crazy."

"Did he lose all his family?"

He nodded. "Fourteen relations, including his wife and three children. He's the sole survivor. The thing is, he doesn't want compensation. We've already sent him quite a large sum. He just put it in a drawer."

"What, then?"

He raised his eyebrows ironically. "He wants them to understand what they've done," he said. "Only that."

There was a knock at the door of the outer office, and a boy appeared with sandwiches. Konrad divided them between two paper plates with a napkin on each.

"Well, now," he said as they began to eat, "I've got your ticket. Your plane leaves at nine tomorrow morning. I'll drive you to the airport, of course."

She was taken aback. "But Mama – are you sure Mama will be all right?"

"I told you."

"But what about –?"

"If you mean the business of the Professor's pills which I so stupidly alluded to on the phone, I've persuaded her that she told me about it herself."

"And she believed you?"

He nodded, almost regretfully. "Oh yes," he said. "She believed me."

She felt confused and not entirely reassured.

"It's all right," he said. "Forget you ever told me. It didn't matter anyway. You've made me feel less guilty, and for that I'm grateful."

"And you'll look after her?"

"Of course."

"Because without you –" She still was not quite sure.

"Without me, she can't carry on. I make her feel safe." He sighed. "I make everyone feel safe. Her. Ilse. My wife and daughters. For heaven's sake," he said, "I even make Ilse's mother feel safe."

She laughed a little, uncertain what to say. "What will you do about her?" she asked at last.

"Ilse's mother?"

"No."

"Look," he said, "I can only do my best. I've found her another job. With more pay. She starts in a fortnight."

"And she'll be content with that?"

He was suddenly on the defensive. "It's as I told you," he said. "I can only do my best."

After they had eaten, he got a file from one of the drawers and said in his official voice, "You know of course that your family will be getting compensation. I advised your mother on the claim – perhaps you would like to see."

She had known, but forgotten, and now it seemed somehow incongruous. The file had Papa's name on it, and he saw her looking at it.

"I met him once, you know," he said.

"Really?" She was surprised.

"At a refugee function in London. Of course I didn't know your mother then. I admired him very much."

"Did you?" she said, touched.

"He was so witty and interesting. And the things he knew. And his enthusiasm – just like your mother. They were very good together. Both emotionally and intellectually," said Konrad ponderously, "I have never been in their league."

"But Konrad –"

"No," he said, "I haven't, and I know it. I have no feeling for nature, I'd rather see a Western than opera any day, and these days especially, I get tired."

"But she loves you."

"I know," he said. "I make her feel safe. And that's the most confusing thing of all because, as you may have noticed, I'm really a rather unreliable fellow."

Somehow the words "unreliable fellow" sounded very odd, pronounced in his refugee accent.

"You're not," she said, smiling to make it all into a joke.

He only looked at her.

"But you will look after her?"

"I told you," he said, and opened the file.

They looked at the papers together. There were claims for her and Max's interrupted education and a string of things for Papa: loss of property, loss of earnings – he explained it all, why he had claimed in this way rather than another, and how much money they could expect to get.

"Is there nothing for Mama?"

He bristled slightly, thinking that she was criticizing. "She claims in your father's name," he explained. "As his widow, all this money will come to her. It should help her quite a bit. Why? Should there be something? Is there something she should have claimed for that she didn't tell me?"

"I don't know." She felt suddenly silly. "Loss of confidence?"

"*Nu*," He threw up his hands. "If one could claim for that, we'd all be claiming."

He insisted on coming down in the lift with her to get her a taxi, and as they went out through the big glass doors of the building, they met Ilse coming in. She was carrying a Thermos flask and looked flustered when she saw them.

"You've already eaten," she cried. "And I'd got you this. It's from home – they filled it up with coffee for me across the road."

"Wonderful," said Konrad. "I'll drink it in a minute."

"You need it, this weather," said Ilse. "I've got some sugar in my pocket. And I know where I can borrow a proper china cup."

She smoothed the Thermos with her hand, looking house-proud and faintly self-satisfied, and Anna suddenly knew of whom she reminded her. Apart from being so much younger, she looked remarkably like Konrad's wife.

It was even colder when she got out of the taxi at the hospital, and she had to wait a few minutes before seeing Mama.

"Sister is with her," said the nurse, and when she finally went in, she found Mama sitting up in a chair. She was wearing the flowered dressing-gown she had bought soon after going to Germany and was making some kind of a list. Even though it was only early afternoon, the day had become very dark, and in the light of the table lamp Mama looked frailer than she had done in bed.

"They want to move me to the convalescent home next week," she said. "And then I'll be going away with Konrad. I must organize my clothes."

"So everything's all right."

"Oh yes." But Mama still looked jumpy. "It was just this silly business of Erwin's illness. And Konrad – I do realize all this has been a great strain on him. And of course he's having a lot of trouble with the German girl. He's found her another job, you know."

"Yes," said Anna.

"He's booking our hotel this afternoon. It's right up in the mountains. We've been there before – it should be lovely."

"That's good."

"And the sister thinks I should practise getting up a bit, especially as I'm going to the convalescent home." Suddenly her eyes had filled with tears and she was crying again.

"Mama – what is it, Mama?" Anna put her arms round her, finding her somehow smaller than she used to be. "Don't you want to go to the convalescent home? Isn't it all right?"

"Oh, I think it's quite nice." Mama blinked and sniffed. "It's just – the thought of the change. Of moving again. The sister says it's got a ping-pong table," she said through her tears.

"Well, you'll like that."

"I know. I'm just being silly." She rubbed her eyes. "I think this kind of poisoning – it is a kind of poisoning, the doctor said so – it leaves one rather confused. Do you know, Konrad was talking about something I once told him, and I could remember absolutely nothing about it. I mean, I couldn't remember telling him. Anyway –" She sniffed again – "It didn't really matter."

"I'm sure it didn't."

"No. Well, anyway, I'd better have some things washed and cleaned." She wrote something more on her list. "I thought I'd ask Hildy."

"Mama," said Anna, "when you come back from your holiday – if you're still not quite all right, or if you just suddenly feel like it – why don't you come to London?"

"To London?" Mama looked alarmed. "What should I do in London? Anyway, I'm coming to London at Christmas, aren't I?"

"Yes, of course. I only thought, if you suddenly got fed up –"

"Oh, I see. You mean, if things don't work out with Konrad."

"Not necessarily –"

"If things don't work out with Konrad," said Mama, "I'm certainly not going to hang round your and Max's necks."

There was a pause. Anna could see something drifting slowly down outside the window. "I think it's trying to snow," she said. They both watched it for a moment.

"Look, Mama," she said at last. "I'm sure everything will be fine with Konrad. But if by any chance it weren't, it wouldn't be the end of the world. I mean, you'd still have Max and me, and your job if you want it, or you could easily get one in another part of Germany. You've done it lots of times before."

"But it would be different now."

"Well, it's never quite the same, but – look, Mama, I'm not a child. I do know what it's like." Suddenly she remembered with great clarity how she herself had felt, years before, when she had been jilted by a man she loved. "You think that your life is finished, but it isn't. It's awful for a while. You feel that nothing is any good, you can't bear to look at anything or to listen to anything or even to think of anything. But then, especially if you're working, it gradually gets better. And you meet new people, and things happen, and suddenly, though life perhaps isn't as good as it was, it's still quite possible. No, really," she said, as Mama seemed about to interrupt, "for someone like you, with an interesting job, and no money worries, and us –"

"You've described it very well," said Mama. "But there is one thing you don't know. You don't know how it feels to be fifty-six years old."

"But I can imagine."

"No," said Mama. "You can't. It's quite true, I could do all the things you say. But I don't want to. I've made enough new starts. I've made enough decisions. I don't want to make any more. I don't even," said Mama, her mouth quivering, "want to go to that bloody convalescent home with the ping-pong table."

"But that's because you're not well."

"No," said Mama. "It's because I'm fifty-six, and I've had enough."

The snow was still drifting past the window.

"One of the doctors was talking to me yesterday," said Mama. "You know, they have all this awful psychology now, even in Germany. He thinks that when someone tries to kill themselves, it's a cry for help – that's what he called it. Well, all I know is that when I had swallowed those pills, I felt completely happy. I was lying on my bed – they take a while to work, you know – and it was getting dark outside, and I was looking at the sky and thinking, there's nothing I need to do. It no longer matters. I'll never, ever, have to make another decision. I've never in my life felt so peaceful."

"Yes, but now – now that everything's changed and you're going on holiday and –" Anna had a little difficulty in getting this out – "if everything is all right with Konrad, won't you be quite glad?"

"I don't know," said Mama. "I don't know." She frowned, trying to think exactly what she meant. "If I had died, you see, at least I should have known where I was."

It did not occur to her that she had said anything odd, and she looked surprised when Anna laughed. Then she understood and laughed too. "Why do you always think I'm so funny?" she said delightedly, like a child who has inadvertently made the grown-ups laugh. "I'm really very serious."

Her snub nose stuck out absurdly under her tired blue eyes and she sat there in her flowery dressing-gown, needing to be looked after.

Later the nurse brought them tea with some little cakes. ("*Plätzchen*," said Mama. "Do you remember how Heimpi used to make them?") Konrad rang up to say that he had booked the hotel and also to remind Anna that he would pick her up early next morning.

After this, Mama went happily back to bed and, even though it was now quite dark outside, they left the curtains drawn back, so that they could watch the snow. It was too wet to stick, but of course, said Anna, it would be different in the Alps. Mama asked about her new job and, when Anna explained about it, said, "Papa always said that you ought to write." She only spoiled it a little by adding, "But this job is just for television, isn't it?"

Towards seven, the sister came back and said that Mama had had a very tiring day, and Anna shouldn't stay too long. After this, it became more difficult to talk.

"Well –" said Anna at last.

Mama looked up at her from the bed. "It's been so nice today," she said. "Just like the old days."

"It has," said Anna. "I've enjoyed it too."

"I wish you could stay longer."

Instant panic.

"I can't," said Anna, much too quickly. "I've got to get back to my job. And Richard."

"Oh, I know, I know," said Mama. "I only meant –"

"Of course," said Anna. "I wish I could stay, too."

She finally left her with the nurse who had brought in her supper.

"I'll write every day," she said as she embraced her.

Mama nodded.

"And look after yourself. And have a lovely time in the Alps. And if you suddenly feel like it, come to London. Just ring us up and come."

Mama nodded again. "Goodbye, my darling," she said, very moved.

Anna looked back at her from the door. She was leaning back in the bed as she had so often done in the Putney boarding house, her grey hair spread on the pillow, her blue eyes brave and appallingly vulnerable, her nose ridiculous.

"Goodbye, Mama," she said.

She was almost out of the room when Mama called after her, "And give my love again to Max."

She came out of the hospital for the last time and suddenly didn't know what to do next. The snow was trying to stick. It glistened patchily on the invisible grass and, more thinly, in the drive, making a pale shine in the darkness. A taxi drew up, white flakes whirling in the beam of its head-lamps, and deposited a woman in a fur coat.

"*Wollen Sie irgendwo hin?*" asked the driver.

It was not yet eight o'clock, and she could not face going back to the hotel. "*Ja, bitte,*" she said, and gave him the Goldblatts' address.

She found Hildy in a state of euphoria. Erwin was much better and the doctor, who had only recently left, had assured her that he was suffering not from hepatitis but the current form of mild gastric 'flu.

"So we are celebrating with cognac," she said, handing Anna a glass. "We are drinking to the hepatitis which did not catch him."

"And also to the brave Hungarians who have defied the Russians," Erwin called through the half-open door. She could see him sitting up in bed, a glass of cognac in his hand, the billowing quilt covered with newspapers which rustled every time he moved.

"Look at this," he cried. "Have you seen it?"

"Ach, poor Anna, from one invalid to the next," said Hildy, but he was holding out the illustrated paper so eagerly that she went in to see. It showed a fat, frightened man emerging from a house with his hands above his head. "Hungarian civilians arrest a member of the hated secret Police," said the caption. In another picture, a secret policeman had been shot and his notebook which, the caption explained, contained the names of his victims, had been left open on his chest. There were pictures of dazed political prisoners released from jail, of children clambering over captured Russian tanks, of the Hungarian flag, the Russian hammer and sickle torn from its centre, floating over the giant pair of boots which was all that was left of Stalin's statue.

"What they have done!" said Erwin. "What these wonderful people have done!" He raised the cognac to his lips. "I drink to them," he cried, and emptied his glass, which Anna felt sure could not be good for him. But she too was moved, and glad for a moment to think of something other than Mama.

She smiled and emptied her glass also. It was surprising how much better she felt almost at once.

"Wonderful," murmured Erwin and was refilling both of them from the bottle on his bedside table, when Hildy took over.

"So now it's enough," she said. "You'll only give her your germs."

She took the bottle and carried both it and Anna off to the kitchen, where she was in the middle of chopping vegetables for soup.

"And so," she said, as she settled Anna on a stool. "What's new?"

Anna was not sure where to start. "I'm going home tomorrow," she said at last.

"Good," said Hildy. "and how is your Mama?"

The fumes from the cognac mingled with the fumes from Hildy's chopped onions, and she was suddenly tired of pretending.

"I don't know," she said, looking hard at Hildy. "All right, I suppose, if Konrad stays with her. If not . . . I don't know what will happen if he doesn't."

Hildy looked back at her equally hard.

"So what are you going to do about it?" she said. "Stick them together with glue?"

"Of course not. But –" She wanted desperately to be reassured. "It seems awful to leave her," she said at last. "But I can't bear to stay. And I think I've really made it worse by being here. Because I told Konrad – I told him something about Mama. He says it didn't matter, but I think it did."

Hildy swept the onions into a saucepan and started on the carrots. "Konrad is old enough to know if it mattered or not," she said. "And your mother is old enough to know if she wants to live or die."

It seemed an absurd over-simplification, and Anna felt suddenly angry. "It's not as easy as that," she said. "It's easy to talk, but it's not the same as coping with it. I think that if your mother had tried to kill herself, you'd feel very different."

There was a silence because Hildy had stopped chopping. "My mother was not at all like yours," she said. "She was not so clever and not so pretty. She was a big woman with a big Jewish nose who liked to grow *Zimmerlinden* – you know, house plants. There was one that she'd grown right round the living-room window, she called it '*die grüne Prinzessin*' – the green princess. And in 1934, when Erwin and I left Germany, she refused to come with us because, she said, whoever would look after it?"

"Oh, Hildy, I'm sorry," said Anna, knowing what was coming, but Hildy remained matter of fact.

"We think she died in Theresienstadt," she said. "We're not quite sure – there were so many, you see. And perhaps you're right, what I say is too simple. But it seems to me your mother is lucky, because at least she can choose for herself if she wants to live or die."

She went back to chopping the carrots. Anna watched the glint of the knife as they collapsed into slices.

"You see, what are you going to do?" said Hildy. "Go to your mother each morning and say, 'Please, Mama, live another day?' You think I haven't thought about my mother, how I should have *made* her come with us? After all, she could have grown *Zimmerlinden* also in Finchley. But of course we did not know then how it would be. And you can't make people do things – they want to decide for themselves."

"I don't know," said Anna. "I just don't know."

"I'm a few years younger than your mother," said Hildy. "But she and Konrad and I – we're all the same generation. Since the Nazis came, we haven't belonged in any place, only with refugees like ourselves. And we do what we can. I make soup and bake cakes. Your mother plays bridge and counts the miles of Konrad's car. And Konrad – he likes to help people and to feel that they love him. It's not wonderful, but it's better than Finchley, and it's a lot better than Theresienstadt."

"I suppose so."

"You don't suppose – you know. Anyway, what can you do about us? Make the Nazis not have happened? You going to put us all back in 1932? And if your mother, with her temperament, says this life is not good enough for her, you going to make her go on living whether she wants to or not?"

"I don't know," said Anna again.

"She doesn't know," said Hildy to the carrots. "Look, can't you understand, it's not your business!" She swept the carrots into the pan with the rest and sat down at the table. "You want something to eat?"

"No," said Anna. "I mean, thank you, I'm not hungry."

Hildy shook her head. "Pale green, you look."

She picked up the cognac and filled up her glass. "Here, drink. And then home to bed."

Anna tried to think how many glasses of cognac she had already had, but it was too difficult, so she drank this one as well.

"I would just like –" she said, "I would just like to know that she will be all right."

"*Nu*, that you know. Konrad is a good man, and they have been together so long. He will certainly stay with her, at least for a while."

"And then?"

"Then?" Hildy raised both hands in the age-old Jewish gesture. "Who can worry about then? Then, what do we know, everything will probably be quite different."

It was snowing more than ever as the taxi drove her home to the hotel. She leaned back, dazed, and looked out at the flickering whiteness racing past the window. It shone when caught by the light, broke up, whirled, disappeared, touched the window from nowhere and quickly melted. You could see nothing beyond it. You might be anywhere, she thought.

Her head swam with the cognac she had drunk, and she pressed it against the glass to cool it.

Perhaps out there, she thought, is a different world. Perhaps out there, as Hildy said, it really had, none of it, ever happened. Out there Papa was still sitting in the third row of the stalls, Mama was smiling on the beach, and Max and the small person who had once been herself were running up some steps, shouting, *"Ist Mami da?"*

Out there the goods trains had never carried anything but goods. There had been no torchlight processions and no brown uniforms.

Perhaps out there Heimpi was still stitching new black eyes on her pink rabbit. Hildy's mother was still tending her plants. And Rachel Birnbaum, aged six, was safe at home in her bed.

Friday

She woke early and was out of bed and at the window almost before she had opened her eyes, to see what the weather was like. It had worried her, at intervals during the night, that the plane might not be able to take off in heavy snow. But when she looked out into the garden, most of it had already melted. Only a few shrinking patches were left on the grass, pale in the early morning light. The sky looked clear enough – grey with some streaks of pink – and there seemed to be little wind.

So I'll get away all right, she thought. She wrapped her arms about her against the cold and suddenly became aware of feeling rather strange. I can smell the glass, she thought. I can smell the glass of the window. At the same time, her stomach gave a heave, everything rose up inside her, and she just managed a wild rush to the basin before she was sick.

It happened so suddenly that it was over almost before she knew it. For a moment she stood there shakily, letting the water run from the taps and rinsing her mouth in the tooth-glass. This is not tension, she thought. Oh God, she thought, I've caught Erwin's gastric 'flu. Then she thought, I don't care – I'm still going home.

She was afraid that if she once went back to bed, she might stay there, so very slowly and methodically, she put on her clothes, opened her suitcase, threw in her things, and then sat down in a chair. The room was inclined to rise and sink around her, but she made a great effort and kept it steady.

Perhaps, after all, it was only the cognac, she thought. She kept her eyes focused on the curtains, mercifully still today, and concentrated on their intricate, geometrical pattern. Gradually, as she followed the interlocking woven lines on the dark background, the nausea receded. Down, across, down. Across, down, across. In a moment, she thought, I'll be able to go and have some breakfast.

And then she suddenly realized what she was looking at. The pattern resolved itself into a mass of criss-crossing right-angles. It consisted of nothing but tiny, overlapping swastikas.

She was so surprised that she got up and walked across to them. There was no doubt about it. The swastikas were woven right through the fabric. Her nausea forgotten, she was filled instead with a mixture of amusement and disgust. I always thought that woman was a Nazi, she thought. She had found swastika patterns in Germany before, of course – engraved on the cutlery in a restaurant, carved deep into the backs of chairs or into the newspaper holders in a café. But she was repelled by the thought that she had unwittingly shared a room with this one, that she had been looking at it while thinking about Mama and Papa.

It's just as well I'm leaving, she thought. She moved her eyes from the curtains to the window and, very carefully, turned round. Then she walked down to the breakfast room and drank two cups of black coffee, after which she felt better. But the table was grubby as usual, a German voice was shouting in the kitchen, and suddenly she could not wait to get out of the place.

She went to fetch her suitcase and put on her coat. The proprietress, to her relief, was nowhere about, so she did not need to say goodbye to her. She smiled at the adolescent girl who, she calculated, could not have been more than three or four at the end of the Thousand Year Reich and could not thus be held responsible. Then she carried her suitcase out into the street and, even though it was far too early, sat on it in the cold until Konrad arrived to collect her.

"You look terrible," he said as they stood together at the airport. "What's the matter with you?"

"I think I had too much cognac last night.

I felt awful when I first got up, but I'm all right now."

It was not strictly true. She was still troubled by nausea, coupled with the curious intensification of her sense of smell. The leather seats of Konrad's car had been almost too much for her, and she had ridden a large part of the way with her nose stuck out of the window.

"I'm quite well enough to travel," she said, suddenly afraid that he might somehow stop her.

"I wouldn't dream of daring to suggest otherwise," he said. "Especially as I've cabled Richard to meet you."

She smiled and nodded.

There was a pause. She could smell his coat, floor polish, a packet of crisps which someone was eating, and the wood of some seats nearby, but it was all right – she did not feel sick.

"Well," he said. "This is very different from when you arrived. At least we've got your mother through."

"Yes." She hesitated. "I hope it won't be too difficult for you now. With – with your secretary and everything."

"I'll manage," he said. "Obviously, one can't just – abandon people. But I'll manage."

"And I hope you have a good time in the Alps."

"Yes," he said. "I hope so too."

"And when you come back –" She suddenly needed, desperately, to hear him say it – "you will look after Mama, won't you?"

He sighed and smiled his tired, asymmetrical smile. "You should know me by now," he said. "I always look after everybody."

There was nothing more she could say.

The smell of crisps became suddenly overwhelming and nausea returned, but she fought it down.

"Good luck with the job," said Konrad. "I look forward to seeing your name on the television screen. And give my love to Richard."

"I will."

"Perhaps I'll see you both at Christmas. I'll be in London then to visit my family."

"That'll be lovely." The part of her not occupied with the crisps noted that it was ludicrous of him to mention his family at this point, but replied, even more ludicrously, "And Mama will be there then as well."

They looked at each other and then, to her relief, her flight was called.

"Goodbye," she cried and, on an impulse, embraced him. "Look after yourself. And thank you!"

"For what?" he called after her, and it was true, she did not know. For making Mama happy in the past? For promising, with no great certainty, to look after her in the future? Or just because she herself was at last going home?

She turned and waved to him from Passport Control and he waved back. Then she watched him thread his way through the crowd in the lounge – a tall, fat elderly man with thinning hair and a stick. The great lover, she thought and it seemed very sad.

She was almost sick again as the plane took off – but here at least, she thought, they'll just think it's air sickness. She got as far as feeling for the paper bag provided, just in case, but as the plane rose up into the sky, away from the rubble and the re-building, from the dubious goods trains and the even more dubious people who claimed to have known nothing about them, away from the threatening Russians and the ex-Nazis whom they so much resembled, from the Grunewald and the German language and Mama and all her problems, it seemed as though her nausea had been left behind with all the rest.

She looked out at the blazing sky and felt a huge sense of relief. Well, I've made it, she thought, as though it had been some kind of escape. She was suddenly hungry, and when the stewardess brought her some breakfast, she devoured a double portion, to the last crumb. Afterwards she wrote a note to Mama, to be posted at London Airport. This way, she thought, Mama would get it tomorrow and it would be something, at least, to stave off depression. When she had stuck down the envelope, she leaned back in her seat and stared out at the sky.

"We have now left the Eastern Zone of Germany and are flying over the Western Zone," said the stewardess through a little microphone. "In a few minutes you may see the city of Bremen on your left."

The man beside her, a middle-aged American, stirred and smiled. "I guess it's silly of me," he said, "but I'm always glad when we get to this bit."

She smiled back at him. "So am I."

Already, as she looked back, her time in Berlin was beginning to shrink into the past. I didn't do much good there, she thought, but with detachment, as though she were considering someone else. Small, fleeting images ran through her mind – Mama searching for a handkerchief under her pillow; the exact inflection of Konrad's voice as he said, "The affair, of course, is finished." Perhaps one day I'll really write about it, she thought, and this time the idea did not seem so shocking. If I did it properly, she thought – the way it really was. If I could really describe Mama.

But as she picked through everything that had happened, there was a sense of something missing. Something forgotten, or perhaps neglected – something quite ordinary and yet important, that should have happened but hadn't. If I could just remember that, she thought. But she was tired and it was lovely not to feel sick any more, and after a while she put it out of her mind.

What would Papa think about it all? she wondered. During his last years, when her German had faded and Papa's English remained inadequate, they had made a joke of addressing each other very formally in French . . . *Qu'en pensez-vous, mon père?* she thought, and only realized from her neighbour's astonished glance that she must have said it aloud.

"I'm sorry," she said. "I think I was dreaming."

She closed her eyes to make it look more convincing, shutting out everything except the throbbing of the engines. Of course if you wrote about it, you'd have to put all that in, she thought. The different languages and the different countries. And the suitcases. Packed and re-packed so many times. Stored in the lofts and basements of the various shabby boarding houses, counted and re-counted on the train journeys from one temporary home to the next.

"*Wir fahren mit der Eisenbahn*," said Mama. The iron railway. It even sounded like the noise the train made rattling across Germany. The compartment was dirty and Max had got his knees black from searching for his football under the seat. "Here comes the passport inspector," said Mama and put her finger to her lips, so that Anna would remember not to give them away to the Russians. She could see them standing all along the frontier in an endless line.

"Anything to declare?" said Konrad, and she forgot and told him about the Professor's pills, but Mama shouted, "I'm fifty-six years old," and the train moved on, across the frontier, right through the middle of Paris and up Putney High Street.

"I've got the children through," said Mama to Papa who was sitting by his typewriter in his shabby room. He smiled fondly, ironically, and without a trace of self-pity. "As long as we four are together," he said, "nothing else matters."

"Papa," cried Anna, and found herself looking at the face of a stranger. It was quite close to her own, carefully made up and surrounded by permed, blonde hair. Below it was a crisp, blue blouse and a tailored tunic.

"We are about to land at London airport," said the stewardess. "Please fasten your seat belt." She looked at Anna more closely. "Are you quite well?" she said. "You're looking very pale."

"Quite well, thank you." She must have answered automatically, for she was still too much hung about by the dream to know what she was saying.

"Is someone meeting you at the airport?"

"Oh, yes." But for one endless, panicky moment, she could not remember who it was. Papa? Max? Konrad? "It's all right," she said at last. "I'm being met by my husband."

"Well, if there's anything you need –" The stewardess smiled and moved on.

They dived down through the cloud, and below it was raining. Everywhere was wet, and there was mud on the airport floors from the passengers' feet.

UK passports to the right, others to the left. She went through the gate on the right with more than the usual feeling of having conned someone, but the man smiled at her as though she belonged. "Not very nice weather to come home to," he said.

The customs officers in their blue uniforms were easy and relaxed as usual. "What, nothing?" they said. "Not even a bottle of schnapps for the boy-friend?"

"Nothing," she said, and there, beyond the partition, she could see Richard.

He was looking past her at a group of people just coming in, and for a moment she watched him as though he were a stranger. A slight, dark-haired man, carelessly dressed with a quick, intelligent face. English. Well – more Irish really. But not a refugee. He looked alone and unencumbered. He's lived here all his life, she thought. He's never spoken anything but English. Papa died years before I even met him. She felt suddenly weighed down with past words and places and people. Could she really belong with anyone so unburdened?

The customs officer made a white chalk mark on her suitcase, and at the same moment Richard turned and saw her.

"Anna!"

She grabbed her case and ran towards him. As she reached him, she saw that he looked tired and worried. She dropped the case and fell into his arms. He smelled of coffee, paper and type-writer ribbons.

"Darling," she said.

He said, "Thank God you're back."

For the first time since she'd left him, she felt all of one piece. There were no more doubts. This was where she belonged. She was home.

* * *

"It's been getting a bit frightening," he said, as they sat together on the airport bus.

"The Suez business?"

"And Hungary."

"But I thought that was all right."

He looked astonished. "All right?"

"Settled."

"Haven't you heard? It's in all the papers. You *must* have heard."

"No." But she knew from his face what it was. "Did the Russians –?"

"Of course. When they said they were moving out, they were just waiting for reinforcements. Now they've got them and they've pounced. Tanks all round Budapest. They've grabbed the Hungarian leaders. They're closing the frontiers and chucking out the Western press."

She felt suddenly sick. "So all those people –"

"That's right," he said. "God knows what will happen to them now. Apparently thousands of them are getting out while they can."

Again! she thought, and was overcome by anger. "Surely someone must do something," she said. "They can't just be left."

He said nothing.

"Well, can they?"

He smiled wryly. "The Labour Party are having a huge protest rally in Trafalgar Square."

"About Hungary?"

"About us. How wicked we are, going into Suez like awful imperialists. And while we're busy with our own little fiasco, the real imperialists are doing what they like."

Outside the window of the bus, streets of identical red brick houses streamed past in the rain and were left behind.

"I think everybody's scared," he said. "You can see it in their expressions. It could so easily all blow up."

More houses, a factory, a horse in a scruffy field. What about Mama? she thought. "You think there'll be trouble in Berlin?"

He made a face. "If it did blow up, I suppose it wouldn't matter where you were. But I'm very glad you're back."

"So am I. Oh, so am I."

His coat was damp, and she could smell the tweed, mixing with the rubbery smell of other people's macs.

"Will your mother be all right?" he asked. "I mean, with Konrad?"

"I don't know." She wanted to tell him about it but suddenly felt too tired. "It's very complicated," she said.

"Konrad always seemed so responsible."

"That's the funny thing," she said. "I think he is."

At the air terminal in Kensington High Street the bus deposited them, and they stood on the curb with her suitcase, trying to get a taxi. As usual in the rain, these all seemed to be full, and she stood there in the wet, peering out at the cars and buses splashing past through the puddles, and felt utterly exhausted.

He looked at her in concern. "Are you all right?"

She nodded. "I think I had too much cognac last night. And very little sleep. There's one!" A taxi had appeared round a corner, empty, and she hailed it.

"Poor love," he said. "And you had the curse as well."

The taxi came towards them and she watched it approaching, infinitely slowly. So that's it, she thought – the thing that had been missing, the thing that should have happened in Berlin but hadn't. She could see the driver's face under his woolly cap, the wet shine of the metal, the water spurting from the wheels like a film in slow motion – she could almost count the drops – and she thought, good heavens, me! It's happened to me! The taxi stopped.

"No," she said. "I didn't."

He stared at her. "You didn't?"

"No." She could feel the happiness rising into her face and saw it echoed in his.

"Good God," he said.

The driver watched them from behind the steering wheel. "You do want a taxi?" he asked with heavy irony.

"Of course." Richard gave him the address and they scrambled in.

"Are you sure?" he said. "I suppose it could have been the strain."

"No," she said. "I was sick this morning, too. And there's something else that's funny – I keep smelling things." She felt for the words. "I'm with child."

She laughed with pleasure, and he laughed too. They sat very close together, thinking about it, while the taxi crawled through the traffic. Near Kensington Church Street a policeman stopped them to allow a small procession to cross the road. Middle-aged people, some with umbrellas, carrying placards. "Save Hungary" she read, but there were not many of them and they soon passed. Then up Church Street, down the side streets lined with trees, almost bare now, the sodden leaves clogging the gutters –

"I wonder what it will be," said Richard. "Do you mind which?"

"Not really." But she imagined a daughter. A little girl, running, laughing, talking . . . "I suppose it won't speak any German."

"You could teach it if you liked."

"No," she said. "No, I don't think so." Anyway, it wouldn't be the same.

Much later, when it was getting dark, she sat in the little living-room on the new striped sofa, listening to the news. She had unpacked, and telephoned James Dillon – though now, she supposed, she would only be able to do the new job until the baby was born – and had told Richard all about Mama. She had inspected the dining-room rug which looked just right but might not be suitable for a nursery, and they had decided on Thomas for a boy but had not been able to agree on a name for a girl.

The curtains were drawn, supper was cooking in the kitchen, and apart from the fact that the stack of typewritten sheets next to Richard's typewriter had grown taller, she might never have been away. She could hardly remember Berlin, or even a time when she hadn't known that she was pregnant.

The newsreader's careful accents filled the room. The Egyptian army had been routed, a British cruiser had sunk a frigate, British and French infantry were ready at any moment to move in –

"Are you sure you want to listen to this?" asked Richard anxiously. He had got some glasses from the kitchen and was pouring her a drink.

She nodded, and the careful voice went on. "In Hungary the Russians have swept back in force . . ." He gave her a glass and sat down beside her. ". . . no one knows what will happen now to the brave people of Budapest . . . the Secret Police, wreaking a terrible vengeance . . . refugees, many of them children, pouring across the frontier . . ."

She sipped her drink, but it didn't help.

". . . never again, said a spokesman, will the West be able to trust . . ."

She found that tears were running down her face. Richard reached out, there was a click, and the voice stopped.

"It makes one weepy," she said. "Being pregnant makes one weepy."

"Everything makes you weepy," he said. He raised his glass and said with fierce affection, "To our little creature."

"To our little creature." She wiped her eyes and sniffed. "It's just –" she said – "it's hardly the best time to start a baby, is it?"

"I don't suppose it ever is."

"No, I suppose it isn't."

He put his arm round her. "You'll be a lovely mum."

She was taken aback by the word. "A mum?" she said doubtfully.

He smiled. "A lovely, lovely mum."

She smiled back.

Somewhere very far away, a small person in boots was running up some steps, shouting, "*Ist Mami da?*"

I wonder how I'll do, she thought. I wonder how on earth I'll do.

The Other Way Round
by Judith Kerr

How did it feel in wartime London to be a German refugee? For fifteen-year-old Anna and her family the anxieties were special and horrifying as the Nazis overran Europe. What hope was there for them if Hitler, who had put a price on Papa's head, invaded England? How could they survive not only the bombs but the financial hardships of every day, when neither Mama nor Papa could get a job? How could Max, who looked, sounded and felt English, persuade the Air Force to accept him in spite of his background? And all the time, the only thing that Anna really wanted was to go to art school...

In this book, Judith Kerr describes how the family, introduced in her first novel *When Hitler Stole Pink Rabbit*, lived through the war.

£3.50

When Hitler Stole Pink Rabbit
by Judith Kerr

Anna was only nine in 1933, too busy with her school work and her friends to take much notice of the posters of Adolf Hitler and the menacing swastikas plastered over Berlin. Being Jewish, she thought, was just something you were because your parents and grandparents were Jewish.

But suddenly, Anna's father was unaccountably missing, and shortly after, she and her brother were hurried out of Germany by their mother with alarming secrecy. Then began their rootless, wandering existence as refugees. Their life was often difficult and sad, but Anna soon discovered that all that really mattered was that the family was together.

An outstanding book for readers of ten upwards.

£3.50

Order Form

To order direct from the publishers, just make a list of the titles you want and fill in the form below:

Name

....

Address

....

....

....

Send to: Dept 6, HarperCollins Publishers Ltd, Westerhill Road, Bishopbriggs, Glasgow G64 2QT.

Please enclose a cheque or postal order to the value of the cover price, plus:

UK & BFPO: Add £1.00 for the first book, and 25p per copy for each additional book ordered.

Overseas and Eire: Add £2.95 service charge. Books will be sent by surface mail but quotes for airmail despatch will be given on request.

A 24-hour telephone ordering service is available to holders of Visa, MasterCard, Amex or Switch cards on 0141- 772 2281.

Collins
An *Imprint of* HarperCollins*Publishers*